Riff

Larkspur Book Two

Zoe Piper

Cover: Morningstar Ashley Designs
Professional Beta Reader: Megan Dischinger – Blue Beta Reading
Editor: Penny Tsallos Editing & Proofreading
Proofreader: Corrinne Beehre
Publisher: Apollo8 Publishing

Digital ISBN: 978-1-99-118802-1
Print ISBN: 978-1-99-118803-8

Riff

Cal thought graduating from MIT would set him up for life, but when he's laid off with crippling student debts to pay, he hits rock bottom. Overqualified for nearly every job he applies for, Cal finds himself jumping at the only opportunity offered to him.

Larkspur's lead-guitarist, Seth, doesn't get involved. Tour crew members are off limits, and he isn't around anyone else long enough to start the real relationship he truly wants, so he keeps to himself and plays up his rebel rocker persona. But his resolve is tested as he finds himself drawn to the band's new assistant.

When Cal reveals why he is on tour with them, Seth can't help giving in and acting more like his rash rebel persona instead of the level-headed man he knows he is. When a fake arrangement turns into more, can Seth convince Cal that there's more to him than meets the eye?

PROLOGUE

T he words in the document in front of him looked like English, but Cal couldn't understand them. He scanned them again and frowned. This made little sense. He was an intelligent man. He had a degree from MIT to prove it, yet, somehow....

"Everything is quite straightforward, Mr. Stevens. You just need to sign at the bottom." The slightly condescending tone of the lawyer's voice broke into Cal's consciousness. He looked up to see a familiar look on the older man's features and sighed internally. Some people may celebrate the fact they looked like a twenty-year-old twink, but it meant he was rarely taken seriously, even though he was five years out of college and hardly had time to date.

"I'm sure you're correct, Mr. Harmon. However, I was taught never to sign anything without reading it first, and I have some questions," Cal replied, his voice steady despite the waves of anxiety rolling through him.

"Cal, really, c'mon. It's straightforward, like Phil said," Beck, one of his colleagues, added.

Cal raised an eyebrow at the use of the lawyer's first name. Things certainly weren't as straightforward as everyone seemed to imply.

"So, you and Clive are fine with being dumped by the company we have given everything to for the last four years?"

Beck's skin flushed a deep red, and he looked to Clive desperately. Cal sat up straighter and eyed what he had thought were two of his best friends.

"What's going on?"

"We... ah... I..." Beck stammered. Clive shifted uncomfortably beside him, and they both looked to the fifth person in the room, some HR flunky named Roland.

"Look, Cal, you know how things go in this industry. You have to be ahead of the game, three steps ahead of the competition if you want to be number one," Roland said, leaning forward in his seat. "To do that, we have to evolve and change, and sometimes, there are casualties. It's nothing personal. We just have to keep everything streamlined and costs at a minimum."

Cal stared at him, again doubting his own intelligence because even though he knew what Roland was saying, he didn't *understand* what was being conveyed. At least he knew what was being said. He was just having a hard time accepting it.

"Let me get this straight," he said, holding up a finger when it appeared there would be no further explanation. "I'm the only one from our team being let go. Beck and Clive get to keep their jobs?" He looked at the lawyer, "Do I have that correct?"

"In principle, yes, you do," Harmon blustered. "However, the terms of the contract are very fair, Mr. Stevens."

"Fair? How are they fair? Who else has worked sixty-hour-plus weeks for the last year doing the advanced coding required for the latest release of the number one gaming app? Certainly not some junior staff member with the ink still wet on their degree, if they even *have* a degree." Cal's anger and frustration were like snakes weaving through him, twisting and turning until all he wanted to do was throw something.

"Sometimes, though, Cal, you need to step back and re-evaluate your life and your priorities," Roland said, his tone placating. "You're a great asset to the company and the work you have done on *Runaway Mule* is appreciated, but Systems Corp can't take all the personnel. A lot of those junior staff are being let go, too."

Cal slumped in his seat as the words slammed into him like darts on a board. They really meant it. Cal's mind flashed briefly back over the last five years. He, Beck, and Clive had met when they had been taken on as interns, fresh out of college. The original company they had signed with had been swallowed up by a bigger, brighter firm, as was typical in the industry, but they had stuck together and helped to develop one of the most popular mobile gaming apps since *Angry Birds*. Now Crinkle Media had been bought by a huge multinational conglomerate, and this time there wasn't room for Cal.

"Wow!" he said, staring at Clive and Beck. "I thought we were friends, but obviously, friendship counts for nothing when it comes down to the almighty dollar."

"We are still your friends, Cal," Clive replied with a smile that Cal was sure was meant to be kind, but came off as faintly sinister. "This is best for all of us. You'll feel better after you've slept on it and realize that this really is a good thing."

"Why are you two keeping your jobs?" he asked as the thought suddenly occurred to him.

"I'm afraid Beck and Clive are not at liberty to discuss the terms of their employment," Harmon replied stiffly before either of the other men could.

Cal picked up the contract and read it through again, ignoring the muted sighs of impatience from the others in the room. As much as he hated to admit it, Harmon was right. It was a fair contract. Systems Corp didn't have to pay him severance, but they offered six months' salary and waived the non-compete clause.

Fatigue washed through Cal. He'd had enough. Yeah, he could stay and fight and argue, but what was the point? They had made the decision. They didn't want him on the team anymore. Maybe a break from all the politics and bitchiness would do him good. With the pay-out, he could take some time to re-evaluate his life.

Hastily scribbling his name on the last page, he dropped the contract onto the table and pushed back his chair.

"I'd like to say it's been a pleasure, but I'd be lying. I hope everything works out for you."

"Wait. C'mon, Cal. It doesn't mean we can't still be friends," Beck implored.

"Friends? I don't think you know the meaning of the word. Good luck to the both of you. Have a nice life."

With that, he strode from the room, keeping his head as high as possible. He managed to get to his small office with no one stopping him, and for that, he was grateful. He probably would have lost what little self-respect he had left if anyone had spoken to him.

He quickly gathered the few personal belongings he had and dropped them into a box. Balancing his potted plant on top, he took one last lingering glance around the space he'd inhabited for the last four years before quietly turning his back on it all.

Maybe Beck was right. Perhaps this was a good thing, but right now, it felt like his world was ending and he had no idea what was going to happen next.

CHAPTER ONE

Two months later

Cal placed the last box that held his worldly possessions into the corner of the spacious spare room in his cousin's house. His shoulders were tight, not only from moving boxes from his old apartment, but with the tension and stress he had been carrying since he'd been made redundant. His emotions were all over the place; all he wanted to do was find a hole and hide in it. Unfortunately, he could not do that, just like he was unable to pay his rent. He hated that he found himself in this situation. Despite several calls and emails to Systems Corp, he had yet to see any money from his settlement.

He slumped down onto the bed and wondered for the umpteenth time what he'd done wrong in a previous life, for everything seemed to be going wrong for him now.

He'd taken the first ten days of his unemployment to relax and unwind. He hadn't been lying when he said he'd been working sixty-plus hour weeks on the last update for *Runaway Mule,* and he'd enjoyed having lazy sleep-ins and time catching up on missed tv series and books as he'd recharged his batteries.

As he'd headed into week two of his forced time off, he'd started looking for a new job and found the market saturated and his applications rejected because he was overqualified for the advertised roles. He'd chewed through what little savings he had, living as frugally as he always had. Despite being well paid over the last few years, he'd decided to save a minimum amount and tried to pay off as much of his huge student debt as he could. As always, hindsight was a wonderful thing, and it was no good wishing he'd saved more and paid less on his debt. Because of his excellent payment history, he'd been able to arrange a temporary payment deferment, but the increased interest was almost going to set him back to square one.

His cousin, Sarge—who was more like an older brother—had called in one day and found Cal hibernating on his couch after yet another rejection and a pile of unpaid bills sitting on the counter.

Sarge had dragged the whole sorry story out of Cal, and then he had taken charge as only a former Marine could. One quick phone call to his wife, Jax, to tell her the situation, and Cal had found himself in a whirlwind of packing and organization and his most urgent bills paid off. Sarge may be a former Marine, but his wife could have been the Chief of Defense for the way she got things done. Given that she was the personal assistant to Larkspur, one of the world's most successful bands, she knew how to get things done and get them done quickly.

A knock at the door interrupted Cal's thoughts, and Jax's blond head appeared.

"Hey, sweetie. You doing okay?"

Cal smiled wanly at her. "Yeah. Thanks again for taking me in. I... I...."

Jax sat next to him and wrapped an arm around his shoulder.

"Cal, listen. I know you feel like the world is against you at the moment, but everything will work out. I know it will."

Cal sighed and nodded in agreement. Rationally, he knew he would find a job and that this was just a speed bump in his life, but it didn't stop him from feeling like a failure. If it wasn't for the kindness of Sarge and Jax, then he dreaded to think what he would have done.

"I know, Jax, and I really appreciate you and Sarge taking me in like this. I promise, the minute I have a job, I'll look for a new place and pay you back the money you lent me to clear my rent and bills."

"Cal, there's no rush. Honestly, we're more than happy to help. Sarge and I do okay, and if we can't help out family, then what does that say about us?"

"Yeah, but—"

"There is no but, and that is the last time I want to hear anything about it okay?"

Cal nodded reluctantly, and Jax beamed at him before giving him another hug. She really did give the best hugs.

"Now, wash up and come down for something to eat." With a final squeeze, Jax left him, and he shook himself mentally before heading to the small bathroom.

He entered the kitchen just as Sarge was pulling a golden roast chicken from the oven, the scent making his stomach rumble. His cousin grinned at him, and despite his worries, Cal couldn't help but grin back. Sarge may be ten years older, but their mothers were exceptionally close, and Sarge had doted on a young Cal, who in turn had worshipped his older cousin.

"All settled in?" Sarge asked, as he expertly carved the meat.

"Yeah, more or less."

"Well, there's no rush. You're welcome here for as long as you need to be."

"Thanks, Sarge," Cal replied.

The three of them sat at the small table to eat, conversation flowing as they caught each other up on family news.

"So, I know you're looking for a new job," Sarge said, as he pushed his empty plate to one side. He held up a hand as Cal opened his mouth. "No, wait a moment. Just hear me out, okay?"

Cal nodded and took a sip from his water glass.

"I know you love your work, and that you're very good at it, and I know you're not having much luck finding a similar position, right?"

"Yeah. I'm overqualified, or the company is so small they can't afford to pay me what I'm worth. I can take a small salary drop, but I don't want to sell myself short."

"Have you considered doing something else?" Sarge asked.

"What, like slinging burgers or tending bar?" Cal gave a short laugh. "Yeah, I've tried for a couple of those too and had a similar response."

Sarge and Jax shared a look, one that held an entire conversation in just a few seconds. Jax turned her attention to Cal, reaching across the table to lay a hand on his.

"What would you think about coming to work for me for a few months?"

"Work for you?" Cal questioned with a frown.

"Yes. As you know, we're heading out on tour again shortly, and I could do with an extra set of hands."

Cal snorted. "Yeah, right. Come on Jax, you are the most organized person I know. You don't need to fabricate a job just for me. Honestly, just staying here rent-free will be a big help, and I'm sure something will come along soon."

"Callahan Stevens, have you ever known me to lie?" Jax's steely blue stare held him in place. He slowly shook his head. He knew better than to contradict the woman. "So, when I say I need an extra pair of hands for this tour, I mean it."

"But why? You've been looking after Larkspur since Miles signed them. What's so different this time?"

"Did you hear that Mark Sullivan has left the band?" she asked, naming Larkspur's drummer.

"Yeah, I did. But you've found a replacement, haven't you?"

"We have. Kellet James is joining the band. In fact, he and his son, Wil, will be here tomorrow."

"Okay. Still not understanding why you need an assistant?"

"Jamie and Kel formed Larkspur when they were teenagers. Kel is the original drummer, but when Miles offered them the contract seventeen years ago, he didn't sign. Long story short, Mark joined the band when they got here to LA, but Jamie has managed to convince Kel to return to the band."

Jax paused and glanced at Sarge, who nodded encouragingly. "I'm going to be busy helping Kel settle into the band and ensuring he's not overwhelmed by everything. Miles and I agreed I need someone I can trust to delegate to."

"And that someone is you," Sarge said, pushing away from the table and collecting their dinner plates.

"But what would I do? I don't have an admin background. I mean, yeah, I know my way around a computer, but I can't see you needing that much IT support."

"You don't need an admin background, and admittedly, some jobs will be really mundane and entry level—"

"You mean, I'd be the guy who gets your coffee and dry-cleaning," Cal interrupted, his tone dry.

Jax had the grace to blush. "Yeah, sort of, but honestly Cal, I know this is not something you'd normally consider, but look at it this way. You get to travel across North America for the summer with a rock band, and you'll get paid to do it."

"Jax," Cal said with a sigh. "I appreciate the offer, but you guys are doing enough for me. You don't have to create a position just for me. I'll be perfectly fine house-sitting for you both."

"Cal, you're not listening. Regardless of who it is, I'm getting an assistant. I'd just prefer it to be someone I know and can trust from day one. I won't have to tell you six times what I need done.

You're as meticulous and as organized as I am. Cal, I *need* you with me."

Cal could hear the sincerity in her tone. Jax was as honest as the day was long. She didn't suffer fools gladly, and he knew the tours were hard work and that she always came home exhausted. He knew she loved her job and wouldn't have it any other way.

"Okay, I'll do it," Cal agreed, semi-reluctantly. Jax grinned in delight and ran round the table to give him a hug.

"Oh, Cal, thank you."

"Thanks, Cal," Sarge said, joining the hug. "I think time away from LA will do you a world of good. You can keep looking and applying for jobs, but in the meantime, you'll be working and keeping busy."

Cal absorbed the strength and love from their hugs. He knew it was the best offer he was going to get and that Sarge and Jax were just looking out for him. Besides, it would be fun to travel with a rock band. Definitely a new experience. What did he have to lose?

Cal ran his hands through his hair and took a deep breath before knocking on the hotel conference room door. Really, it was ridiculous that he was so nervous. He'd done technical presentations in front of larger crowds than the seven people on the other side of the door. *Yeah, but they weren't members of a successful rock band; a band he'd followed and loved since their first hit.*

He heard Jax call out for him to come in, and he pushed open the door and stepped into the room. Jax smiled at him as he instinctively glanced around the table, blushing when he found five pairs of eyes staring at him with curiosity, causing him to freeze in place.

"The audi... audiologist is here for Mr. James," he managed to stammer out, and he could feel his skin heating as he blushed.

"Perfect timing. Come on in, and I'll introduce you." Jax gave him a smile as she drew him forward. "This is Cal, and he's going to be helping me out on the tour as my assistant."

"Hi, Cal," Jamie Larke, the lead singer, said with a bright smile. "Welcome to the craziness that is Larkspur."

"Yeah, we promise to be gentle with you," Seth said with a flirty grin that had Cal blushing even further as long, suppressed teenage-crush hormones flooded back. Seth Worthington on posters and in music videos was one thing, but to see the man up close had Cal's insides heating. Dark blue, hooded eyes regarded him, a smirk tugging at the corner of a full-lipped mouth. His dirty-blond faux-hawk was messy, as though he'd used minimal product and his fingers to style it.

Jax quickly admonished Seth before telling them that Cal was, in fact, Sarge's cousin and a slither of amusement ran through Cal as Seth paled and slunk low in his chair. His cousin could be scary when he wanted to be, and Cal imagined Seth had been on the wrong side of the former Marine once or twice over the years.

Jax waved him into a nearby seat while she finished up the meeting, and Cal took a moment to gather himself. As well as the four members of Larkspur sitting around the table, there was also a good-looking younger man Jax had introduced as Wil James, the teenage son of the new drummer.

Wil looked a lot like his father, and he caught Cal's eye and sent him a friendly grin. Cal couldn't help but grin back, and his anxiety eased a little. Jax had mentioned that Wil was joining the tour as Kellet's assistant, and it would be nice to have someone near his own age of twenty-six.

Not that the others were that much older than him. Ten years at the most, except for Miles Cartwright, Larkspur's manager and Jax's boss. Miles was easily in his early forties but wore it well, with a trimmed and toned body, a smattering of gray in his hair and a close-cut beard.

Cal glanced at the men around the table. Kellet, the new drummer, was paying close attention to what Jax was telling them. It was clear to see the relationship between father and son, as Wil had his father's curls and wide grin. Next to Kellet was Jamie Larke, the lead singer. Classically handsome, he was sitting awfully close to Kellet, and Cal thought he saw a look of longing on his face as he looked at his bandmate. There was obviously some history there, other than being teenage best friends.

Across the table sat Liam Jones, the bass guitarist. He was nodding at whatever Jax was saying and typing every now and then into his phone. Cal risked a glance at Seth and was startled to see the lead guitarist watching him intently.

Cal could feel himself blushing again but kept eye contact and offered a slight nod. Seth winked at him before returning his attention to Jax.

***

Seth tried to focus on what Jax was telling them about a photo shoot they were doing the following day, but his attention was being dragged away by the young blond twink that had been introduced to them. He ticked all of Seth's boxes, from his short, spiky blond hair to his tight body hidden beneath a cream button-down shirt and tailored gray pants that clung to a perfectly round ass.

If Seth had seen him out in a bar or at one of their concerts, he would have been all over Cal in a heartbeat, but he had two strikes against him; he was Jax's assistant, which meant he was staff and Seth had a strict policy of *not* screwing the crew, and second, he was Sarge's cousin. No way was Seth even going to hint that he may be interested in their bodyguard's relative. That was a death wish just waiting to happen.

He watched as the younger man moved his gaze around the table and as their eyes met, a deep blush stained Cal's fair skin. Seth was pleasantly surprised when Cal held eye contact with him and gave him a small nod. In return, he winked at him before returning his attention to their PA.

"Seth, is there anything you want to add to the rider for this leg?" Jax's question jolted him from his musings, and he gave her a cocky smile.

"Just the usual." He paused as Jax sighed and leaned back in her chair, crossing her arms expectantly. Seth grinned, resting his elbows on the table. "A bottle of Ardbeg Hypernova Single Malt Scotch Whisky, and eighty percent dark chocolate truffles hand-crafted by virgin nuns."

A muffled snort came from the end of the table, and Seth glanced at Cal to find the younger man biting his lip to suppress a grin. Seth raised an eyebrow at him. "Do you find my requests funny, Cal?"

Cal blushed again, and his eyes widened at being singled out. He took a deep breath before replying. "I thought all nuns were virgins?" he squeaked out.

Seth grinned lazily. "Very true, but in this day and age, you never can be too sure."

"If that's all, Seth?" Miles asked, his tone indicating that even if it wasn't, Seth should shut up now.

Seth nodded at their manager. He didn't want to annoy Miles, so he reined himself in and sank back into his chair.

Jax quickly wrapped up the meeting, and Seth pushed himself away from the table. He felt his phone buzz in his pocket. Pulling it out, he sighed when he saw it was his brother calling. He knew he should take the call, but he wasn't in the right head space to deal with his family right now, so he shoved it into his jacket pocket, making his escape.

As he exited the room, Jamie called after him.

"Seth, wait up."

He waited for his bandmate, and they fell into an easy walk down the hall towards the elevators.

"Coffee?" he asked.

"Yeah," Jamie agreed as he stabbed the button to call the elevator.

As they waited, Seth took a long look at Jamie.

"What?"

"Nothing," Seth replied. "It was good of you to offer Kel and Wil a place to stay," he commented, knowing full well why Jamie had offered his house for the out-of-towners.

"Makes sense, that's all," Jamie shrugged, trying to appear nonchalant.

The elevator sounded its arrival, and Seth threw Jamie a smirk as they entered the car. "Oh, no, I agree, it does."

"Fuck off, Seth," Jamie responded, without heat, causing Seth to cackle.

"I mean, they could have stayed with me or even Liam, y'know."

"I know they could have, and God knows you've got more than enough room in your McMansion."

"But you wanted Kel where you can see him."

A dull stain colored Jamie's cheeks, and Seth took pity on his friend. He nudged him with his shoulder. "It's all good. If the love of my life was suddenly back in town and in my life, I wouldn't want him anywhere else either."

"I don't know what's going to happen, Seth. I mean, having Kel back in the band is a dream come true. Mark's a good drummer, but Kel, he's...."

"Yeah, I know. I'm gonna miss Mark, but even just being in the meeting this morning with Kel felt like old times. A buzz I haven't felt in a while."

"Hmm, sure that buzz was from Kel and not from Cal?" Jamie teased.

"Cal? Oh, you mean Jax's new assistant," Seth replied, feigning innocence. "Why would I be getting a buzz from him?"

Jamie just laughed and led the way out of the elevator into the hotel lobby.

"I have no idea, Seth. No idea at all," he replied over his shoulder.

CHAPTER TWO

S eth slowly stood from the crouching position the photographer had them posing in. He leaned against Liam's
shoulder and crossed his arms, staring moodily towards the
camera that was pointed at them. He automatically changed
position, dropping his arms and relaxing his face. He'd done this
so many times over the seventeen years since Miles had signed
Larkspur. It had become second nature, and he needed minimal
direction from the photographer or his assistant.

A break was called, and Seth headed towards the table in
the corner of the spacious studio to grab a bottle of water. He
cracked the lid and let his gaze drift over the room as he sipped
from the cold bottle. He'd prefer a beer, but that would have
to wait until later tonight. As soon as they finished here, they
were meeting at Jamie's for their first rehearsal with Kellet as the
drummer.

Kel had slowly relaxed as the morning had worn on, eventu-
ally laughing and joking as though he hadn't been away for so
long. Kel's son Wil was proving to be a chip off the old block and
reveled in teasing his father just as much as everyone else was.

"Excuse me, S... Seth?"

Seth turned to his right and found Cal standing there, blushing.

"What's up, Cal?" he asked, offering a bright smile, which made Cal blush even more. He tamped down an urge to stroke a finger down the glowing skin. He didn't know why Cal seemed so jumpy around him, but he wanted to do everything he could to relax the guy and make him feel at ease with him.

"Oh, I... I just wanted to let you know I heard your phone buzzing in your jacket pocket, and it happened a couple of times, so I just thought you may need to get it, you know, it may be important... or something."

Cal's voice trailed off, and he glanced at the tablet he had in his hands before darting a glance back up at Seth.

Seth dropped a hand on Cal's shoulder and felt the younger man tense under his touch. He immediately drew back, offering a gentle smile.

"Thanks. I appreciate you letting me know. I doubt it's anything urgent because everyone I'm close to is here, but I'll check it out."

"O... okay, then. I'd better get back," Cal said, hitching a thumb over his shoulder toward where Jax was talking with the photographer.

Seth nodded and surreptitiously tracked Cal's slight figure, his eyes lingering on the pert butt showcased perfectly in dark wash jeans. Jax caught his eye over Cal's head and glared at him. He grinned back and shrugged. *What? He was only human.*

To avoid any further admonishment from their PA, he went to the rack where he'd left his leather jacket and pulled out his phone. He swiped open the screen and groaned when he saw the three missed calls from his brother. He'd better call him back. If he did it now, he could at least be truthful when he told Art that he was working and couldn't talk. It would at least keep his brother off his back for a little while longer.

He pressed his brother's number and strode from the room as the call connected.

"Ah, so you are alive then?" Art Worthington asked in lieu of a traditional greeting.

"I know you think I do nothing but laze around all day, brother of mine, but I am actually working at the moment. So, if this is just a wellness check, I'm here. I'm alive, and you have nothing to worry about."

"Seth, you know better than that," his brother sighed, and Seth could hear a hint of hurt in the words. "I know you work hard. You don't get to be as successful as you are without hard work."

"Yeah, try telling Elaine and Donald that," Seth muttered as the familiar wave of helplessness went through him at the thought of his parent's constant disapproval.

"I have. Numerous times."

"I know you have. Sorry, bro, I'm just a bit stressed. We start rehearsals this afternoon, and it's the first one with Kel back."

"I won't keep you then. I just wanted to check in and give you the quarterly reminder about Aunt Rosemary's bequest."

"Ugh, not now, Art. Honestly, what was the woman thinking putting such an archaic clause in her will?"

Art's familiar laugh took away some of Seth's tension. He and his brother may be complete opposites in everything from looks to careers, but they were close, and his older brother had stood up for him against their parents more than once.

"I honestly don't know. I'm sure she was under the influence of one of her sister's brownies at the time," Art replied, causing Seth to grin.

"Yeah, that'd be like Sunny," he agreed. "Hey, man, I've really got to go, but we'll grab a beer next week, okay?"

"That'd be good, Seth. Stay safe, okay?"

"I will. Talk soon." Seth hung up and dropped his head against the wall he was leaning against. He didn't make as much time for his brother as he should, and now with rehearsals and the tour coming up, he was going to have even less time to see him.

"There you are!"

Seth stood at the sound of Liam's voice.

"Sorry, Art called, and I needed to take it."

"Is everything okay?"

Seth nodded as he strode back towards the studio. "Yeah, the usual shit." He slapped Liam on the back, giving him a big grin. "Come on, let's get this done. Then we can go make some music."

***

Cal squinted at the tablet screen, cursing the program that Jax used to track the bookings and movements for the band. It offended his coding sensibilities, and he was tempted to email the software company to tell them how clunky their system was.

"Aww, man! This game sucks." The plaintive wail from Wil pulled Cal from his own mutterings, and he glanced across the table at the nineteen-year-old.

"What are you playing?" he enquired, happy for the distraction.

"Ugh. *Runaway Mule.* They did an update a few days ago, and now the level is super hard to beat unless you use your lucky horseshoes to buy supply packs. You used to be able to collect so many supply packs per level, but there's only been two this level, and I need six to complete it," Wil explained as he threw his phone down in disgust.

"Really? Lemme see. I haven't been on for months." Cal pulled out his own phone and tapped into the gaming app. The first thing he noticed was the change in the opening screen and to his practiced eye, it looked like a poor imitation of the original game. What had Systems Corp done?

"Do you play?"

"Hmm? Oh, yeah. Occasionally," Cal responded as he tapped through the app. He could see some of the updates he'd worked on had been released, but not all of them, which made little sense because they worked better together. Add in the fact that you now had to do in-app purchases to achieve what had previously been free, it looked like Systems Corp was trying to destroy the number one game of the company they'd bought.

"It's a great game—at least it was—before they started doing all these changes," Wil said as he picked his phone up again.

"Thanks," Cal replied distractedly as he tried to get his runaway mule to safety through a swamp.

"Thanks? What am I thanking you for?"

Cal's mule died, and he swiped out of the game. "Oh, I was one of the developers that worked on it for the last few years."

"Wow! Really. That's so cool," Wil exclaimed excitedly. "So how come you left? What are you doing here?"

"Oh, the original company got bought out by Systems Corp and they didn't want me anymore."

"That sucks! So why aren't you working for someone else? Surely with your experience, you'd be able to pick any job you wanted."

"Sadly, it doesn't work like that, or at least for me it hasn't," Cal replied ruefully. "Too many people in the market and not enough jobs. I was lucky that Jax offered me this job, even if it's nothing like I'm used to."

"Hey, the chance to go on tour with Larkspur is nothing to be sneezed at."

"Well, it's certainly something different," Cal agreed with a smile. He liked the bubbly teenager and couldn't help being infected with his enthusiasm. "You must be pretty proud of your dad?"

"Yeah, I am. It took a lot of convincing from my moms and me, though. He can be stubborn, but he caved once Jamie offered me a job too while Mom and Ma are on holiday in Europe."

"He seems to be fitting in well, though," Cal said, nodding towards where the band were laughing and joking as the photographer snapped away. His eyes were automatically drawn to Seth's tall form, and he bit back a gasp at the sight of the lead guitarist with no shirt on. He greedily drank in the sight of smooth skin overlying defined but not bulky muscles. The twin sleeves of tattoos gracing both arms framed his lean muscular torso.

"Yeah, they were all friends when they were my age," Wil said, drawing Cal's attention away from the flesh on display. All four members of Larkspur had been graced in the looks department, and Cal felt a little intimidated.

"Oh, really?" Cal responded, focusing on Wil. *Must not look at the hunky men*. A burst of laughter had his eyes swinging back to the group.

"So, which one do you have a crush on then?" Wil asked in amusement.

"Huh? What?"

Wil chuckled. "You keep staring at them like a hungry dog. Which one do you think is hot?" The teenager's face morphed into a frown. "Oh God, don't tell me you like my dad? That would just be too weird."

"What? No! I don't like your dad. Wait, that came out wrong. I mean, I like your dad, he's a nice guy. But eww, no, I don't think he's hot." Cal could feel himself blushing. Could he be any more awkward? "They're all nice guys, and all have great bodies." At Wil's grin, Cal groaned and dropped his head into his hands.

"S'alright, Cal. I won't say anything. I suppose if I looked at it from your point of view, I could see how you'd think they're hot. But just for the record, don't go crushing on Jamie. He's taken, even if he doesn't know it yet."

"Taken?"

"Yeah, he and my dad were teenage sweethearts but broke up when Miles signed the band. Dad decided that staying behind to raise me was more important than being with the love of his life. It's been eighteen years, but they're both still crazy for each other. They've just got to figure it out."

Cal tried not to appear shocked. He'd wondered what the story was between Jamie and Kellet when he'd seen them interacting the day before, but Wil's explanation surprised him. He couldn't imagine how hard it must have been for the two men.

"Wow, that's amazing. Do you think they'll get back together?"

"Pretty sure they will, yeah," Wil replied. "Jamie's cool and Dad deserves to be happy."

The younger man's attitude impressed Cal. Few teens would be happy with a parent starting a new relationship.

"What about the rest of your family? Are they okay with your dad being with another guy?"

Wil barked out a laugh. "So not an issue in our family. Mom and Dad both figured out they were gay in high school. I was the result of a drunken prom night experiment. Mom's been with my Ma since I was a toddler. We're just one big happy, gay family. I've got three lots of grandparents and they've always been accepting and supportive."

"You're very lucky," Cal said.

"What about you? What's your family like?"

"Mostly, they are accepting. I came out when I left high school. I've had the odd boyfriend, but nothing long-term."

"Wil, it's time to go."

Kellet's shout across the studio had both Cal and Wil realizing that the shoot had finished. Wil gathered his tablet and phone and stood up.

"Great talking to you, Cal. Wanna hang out sometime?"

"I'd like that," Cal replied with a smile. It would be nice to have a friend over the next few months that wasn't his cousin. "Give me your number, and I'll message you later. Do you play online?"

"Yeah, brought my Xbox with me, and it's all hooked up at Jamie's. I'll buzz you later, and we can connect up."

With a wave, Wil hurried to join his father. Cal wistfully watched Seth's retreating figure. The man was way out of his league, but it was nice to dream.

CHAPTER THREE

A familiar tingle ran through Seth as he and the others strode into Madison Square Garden. It had always been a favorite venue of his to play, and now after several very intense weeks of rehearsals, it was finally opening night of their tour.

Kellet had settled into the band like he'd never been away, and their sound was richer and stronger for having him back. Jamie and Kellet had been slowly rebuilding their relationship, and Seth was happy to see his bandmates working things out, although the unresolved sexual tension between them was starting to get to him.

"Right, guys. Soundcheck in ten minutes and then you're free until a quarter to eight," Jax told them. She fixed Seth with a glare. "And when I say a quarter to eight, I don't mean two minutes to eight. Am I clear?"

"Really, Jax. You shouldn't get so stressed out. It's not good for your health," Seth teased back. Before she could respond, he placed a hand over his heart. "I promise I will be all ready to go at precisely 7.45pm."

Jax made an inelegant sound as she turned her attention to Kellet. "You all good, Kel?"

"Yeah. A few nerves, but I'm good," the drummer reassured her. Seth thought Kel looked a little pale, but hey, the guy was due to play in front of twenty thousand people in a few hours' time.

"Okay, you lot, on stage with you. Let's get this over with."

"Such encouragement, Larry. Have you ever considered going into motivational speaking?" Seth asked their tour manager.

"I've heard cat herding is easier than organizing you guys," Larry shot back. "Now get on the damn stage."

Seth mocked a salute and headed to where Blue, his guitar tech, was waiting for him. With a nod of thanks, Seth dropped the strap over his head and settled his favorite Stratocaster into place. He ran his thumb over the strings, pleased to find it was tuned perfectly.

"Perfect as usual. What would I do without you, Blue?" he asked, as he hooked his in-ear monitors into place.

The Australian grinned back at him. "Let's hope you never have to find out."

Seth gave an answering grin before turning his attention to his bandmates. They were all in position, and the voice of their head sound engineer came through the in-ear monitors. With a quick nod to indicate he was ready, Seth waited for Kellet to count them in before playing the opening chords of *When the Sun Rises*, their first hit.

Twenty minutes later, they were drawing to a close, the sound engineers happy with the readings they were getting. Movement off stage caught Seth's attention, and he glanced to his left to see Cal and Wil. Wil was recording them on his phone, and Seth remembered the kid had been tasked with documenting opening night on the band's social media. Cal had his ever present tablet in his hand and was furiously tapping away on it.

Seth put a flourish into the final riff as Jamie belted out the last lines of the song. Cal glanced up and blushed—as usual—when Seth caught his eye and winked at him. Seth had been trying to get the guy to relax around him over the last few weeks. It stung a little that Cal was more at ease with everyone else, yet still skittish around him. Seth had dialed back his teasing, being nothing more than polite and friendly to Cal. In return, he'd received a few shy smiles. Still, Cal rarely instigated a conversation with him unless it was something Jax needed to know. Although Seth had tried to bury his attraction, he wanted to know the younger man better.

"That was great, guys," Larry called out to them. "Now, go and do whatever it is you do before a show, and I'll see you in a few hours."

Seth handed his guitar over to Blue with a nod of thanks. He headed backstage towards his small dressing room. Each of the guys had their own one, and Seth relished the peace and quiet it afforded him before a concert.

"Um, Seth?" Cal's quiet voice stopped Seth in his tracks.

"Hi, Cal. Did you enjoy the soundcheck?" Seth gave the younger man a friendly smile.

"Oh. Yes. I can't wait to see the show tonight. I mean, I know I'm technically working, but Jax says that we can watch the opening show."

Seth was captured by the excitement shining in Cal's green eyes. There was a slight flush to his skin, but for once, it wasn't from a blush, and it highlighted Cal's fine bone structure.

Cal stared back at him and licked his lips nervously, drawing Seth's attention to their fullness. Heat ran through Seth's veins, and his hand lifted as though to reach out. Cal startled at the movement, breaking the trance they'd fallen into.

"Um, so yeah...." Cal cleared his throat. "Jax sent me to ask if you needed anything?"

You wrapped around me. Seth shook his head to rid the errant thought. Cal must have taken it to be his answer, as he nodded and glanced down at his tablet.

"So, I, um... wasn't able to get the chocolates handcrafted by virgin nuns. However, I did find a small boutique chocolatier that does the most amazing truffles, so I got you those instead."

Seth blinked in surprise. His request was his usual piss-take on the whole rider thing, living up to the rebel persona that he perpetuated. Jax knew he always asked for something outrageous just to be ornery. She never took him seriously, and he never actually expected his random requests to be honored. But it seemed that Cal *had* taken him seriously, and it touched him in a way that nothing had for years.

"And how do you know their truffles are amazing?" Seth asked, keeping his tone light and teasing, not wanting Cal to see just how much it meant to him.

Cal smirked at him, the first time he'd ever done so, and the light of mischief in his eyes took Seth's breath away.

"Well, I wouldn't dare to give you something that wasn't worthy, now would I? I carefully tasted several of their offerings and chose the ones I thought you would like the most," Cal told him with a quirk of his eyebrow.

"And how do you think my tastes run?" Seth couldn't help the way his voice dropped at the implied innuendo. To his surprise, Cal didn't break eye contact, although the familiar dull red flush tinged his skin.

"Judging from your other requirements on your rider, I suspect you prefer darker, more savory tones. The truffles have a hint of sea salt, and they go well with the whisky."

"The whisky?"

"Yes, the Ardbeg Hypernova Single Malt Scotch Whisky you also requested. Its smoky undertones will pair well with the high cocoa content in the chocolates."

Seth was momentarily taken aback. Cal had gone to a lot of trouble for him, and he couldn't understand why. The guy seemed scared of him, yet here he was, matching boutique chocolates to limited edition whisky. Folding his arms across his chest, he stared at Cal, trying to figure him out. "You're very knowledgeable, Cal. You don't seem the type to be one to indulge in expensive chocolates and alcohol."

"And what do you think I do indulge in?" Cal shot back, surprising the hell out of Seth even more. Seth's interest grew a notch, and he wanted to see more of this side of him. Who was this guy and what had he done with meek and mild Cal Stevens?

Seth tilted his head to the side as his gaze ran the entire length of Cal's body. "To be honest, I wouldn't like to guess. I'm sure you're a man of many hidden surprises."

A bleep sounded from Cal's tablet, making him frown as he glanced at it.

"Oh, Jax is looking for me." His gaze returned to Seth's, a hint of disappointment in his eyes. He was obviously enjoying the bantering between them, too. "If you don't want me for anything else, I'll leave you to get ready for the show."

"Oh, I want you for many things, Cal," Seth drawled, unable to help himself. "But Jax takes priority."

"Okay, then. If you do, just send a message, and I'll come." As the younger man turned away, Seth caught a hint of a grin and groaned internally at the maybe not-so-unintentional innuendo. It was all he could do to nod and wave before striding quickly to his dressing room. As the quiet encompassed him, he breathed a sigh of relief as he leaned against the door, closing his eyes, trying to get himself under control. Images of Cal, naked and pale, flashed through his head. He could see the fine flush that would engulf Cal's skin as he threw his head back, muscles taut as he came while riding Seth's cock.

Seth groaned and clenched his fists to stop himself from undoing his zipper and taking himself in hand. The sound of his brother's ringtone quickly deflated his semi, and he'd never been so glad for his brother's timing.

"Yeah?" he answered, moving away from the door and dropping onto the small, but very comfy couch, adjusting himself as he did.

"Bad time?" Art asked.

"Nah, all good," Seth said with a sigh. "What's up, Art?"

"Just calling to wish you a good show. Bummed I can't be there for you, but I have a case in two days that I have to prepare for."

"S'all good," Seth reassured him, although he was disappointed his brother wouldn't be there.

"I'll definitely be at the final show, though," Art promised. "And if I can make one of the mid-tour dates, I will."

"Just let me know. There are always a couple of tickets for you, you know that."

"Thanks, little brother. So, everything working out with Kel?"

Seth stretched across the couch, getting comfortable. "Yeah. It's like he's never been away."

"I'm glad. I won't keep you from your pre-show routine, but I just wanted to touch base."

"Thanks, man. I appreciate it," Seth replied. "I'll call you in a few days when we get to Philadelphia."

"Take care, man. Love you, and I'm proud of you."

Before Seth could respond, his brother had hung up. His brother's words warmed him, as they always did. If only their parents felt the same way.

Brushing the thoughts away, his mind drifted back to Cal. Their conversation had been a surprise; it seemed that Cal was learning to relax around him, after all. Seth had enjoyed the gentle teasing and wondered what he could do to see more of it.

Dropping his phone onto the small table in front of the couch, he sighed and scrubbed his hands over his face. He didn't have time to dwell on perky young management assistants with suspected crushes. He was due on stage in a few hours and needed to get into the zone.

He crossed to the table that was laid out with all his favorite foods. He didn't like a heavy meal before performing, and over the years, he and the catering team had come up with a range of healthy, filling snacks that he grazed on during the afternoon. Seth smiled when he saw the beautifully boxed truffles and the bottle of whisky, making a mental note to drop them into his bag to take back to the hotel for after the show.

He fixed himself a plate of cold cuts, crackers, and fruit before grabbing two bottles of water. He set everything on the low table in front of the couch before grabbing a worn leather bag from the corner.

It looked like an oversized briefcase, rectangular in shape, about three feet long and half as wide, and six inches deep. Scuffed along the edges from years of use, the dark tan leather was soft beneath Seth's fingers as he ran a loving hand over the surface. The brass plate with his initials engraved on it looked a little dull, and he gave it a cursory polish with his sleeve, more out of habit than to actually brighten it.

Dropping back onto the couch, his nimble fingers swiftly turned the combination locks to the correct sequence, and the locks popped with a satisfying snap. Settling the case on his lap, his shoulders relaxed as he viewed his art supplies neatly resting in their assigned compartments.

The case had been custom made for him as a gift from his brother for his eighteenth birthday. A quiet beacon of support that helped Seth through the battles with his parents as they fought about their expectations of how Seth should live his life rather than helping and encouraging him to follow his dreams.

He lifted the internal shelf out and pulled out a new sketch-book from the compartment below. There were several there, all fresh and waiting for him to use. By the end of the tour, the compartment would be filled with sketches and drawings, some complete, others merely doodles. It was a ritual he'd started on their first tour, documenting scenes from places they'd visited and quick caricature sketches of his bandmates and the crew.

Now it was a familiar routine that grounded him before a show. He rarely thought about what he was drawing, letting his hand guide the pencil across the page.

He selected two standard pencils and an eraser before closing the case back up. He'd learned the hard way not to leave it undone when the tour bus had suddenly braked one day and his case had slid from one end to the other, scattering its contents along the way.

He could use the lid as an easel if he was doing a particularly intricate piece, but today was just about mindlessly sketching and doodling to calm his mind. He took a few bites of food before settling into the corner of the couch with his feet up on the cushions and opened the sketch pad to the first page.

The scent of fresh paper, overlaid with a hint of the binding glue, had him sighing appreciatively. He brushed away non-existent dust before resting the tip of the pencil against the page. Closing his eyes, his mind wandered as images flitted past his eyelids as he worked out what to sketch.

His hand began to move, and he opened his eyes and gently traced a soft curve, the lead scratching as it glided across the paper. He soon lost himself in the familiar movements, and the shouts and general hubbub of noise as the crew finished setting up faded into the distance.

The chime of his preset alarm had him jerking back to reality. He dropped the pencil into his lap and stretched out his aching fingers before holding the pad up. Wide eyes stared back at him, and a jolt went through him at the likeness of Cal. *Damn it, the man was on his mind more than he realized.*

His finger traced over the arch of Cal's brow. It wasn't quite right, and he itched to trace the real version so he'd get it right next time. *Next time?* A disgusted groan broke from him, and he closed the cover on the sketch pad and stood up from the couch. He really was too hung up on Cal. He couldn't go there. In all his years in Larkspur, he'd stuck to his rule of not messing around with anyone he worked with. Sure, it went against the typical rockstar image he cultivated, and he'd had his fair share of hookups with fans and groupies, but never with anyone closely affiliated with the band. It had been something Miles had drilled into them from day one, and Seth liked and respected Miles too much to disappoint him like that.

He tidied away his art supplies before neatly returning his dirty plate to the corner of the table and dropping his empty water bottles into the recycling can. After freshening up in the small washroom, he picked up his old, battered acoustic guitar to warm up on. He reset the timer so he wouldn't miss Jax's deadline and then lost himself to the familiar chords.

CHAPTER FOUR

C al watched awestruck as Larkspur performed in front of
a capacity crowd at Madison Square Garden. He'd come
to know the guys quite well over the last few weeks, but seeing
them doing their job, consummate professionals, had him realizing just how talented they were.

His glance flicked to Kellet, who, despite his earlier panic
attack before going on stage, seemed relaxed and at home behind his drum kit. His gaze was drawn back to where Jamie was
leaning against Seth as the lead guitarist worked his way through
a complicated riff.

A fine sheen of sweat lit Seth's shoulders and biceps, the
stage lights highlighting the muscle definition shown off in the
sleeveless tee. Worn jeans lovingly hugged Seth's long legs, but
the fast-flying fingers moving along the fretboard had Cal imag-
ining what they would feel like on his body.

He was pulled from his distractions by a nudge in his side.

"Pretty hot, huh?" Wil said with a teasing smile.

Cal nodded without thought, his head moving of its own
accord.

"Ha! Knew you liked him."

"What's not to like?" Cal replied absently, still focused on the way Seth's muscles rippled under the bright stage lights. "He's the epitome of a bad boy rock star. Every gay man's wet dream."

"Wet dreams? At your age, Cal?"

Wil's snort of amusement pulled Cal out of his reverie, and he felt himself blush but couldn't help grinning as his young friend cackled next to him.

"It's alright, you're allowed to crush on the hot rockstar...."

"As long as it's not your dad, yeah, I know," Cal said with a laugh. He nodded towards Kellet. "He seems okay now."

A worried frown crossed Wil's face as he watched his father. "Yeah. I've never seen him like that. Scared me."

"Scared us all. I'm glad Jamie was able to calm him down, though. You might have had to go in his place if he hadn't."

"Hell, no. I mean, don't get me wrong, playing up there would be amazing, but not for me."

A wave of noise hit them as the crowd cheered and screamed their approval at whatever antics the band was up to, and Cal returned his attention to the stage. Seth was taking a drink from a water bottle stored at the base of the drum kit and as he drank, he caught Cal's eye. With a filthy grin, he strutted to the front of the stage, and raced through the opening chords to Larkspur's latest hit before Kellet jumped in on drums. Jamie's voice started as a low growl before almost being drowned out by the crowd joining in.

Cal still couldn't believe he was here. It may not have been in his plans, but he was enjoying his time, and he was grateful to Jax and Sarge for making the opportunity happen.

He checked the time on his tablet, noting that they were only slightly behind schedule. The band had two more songs and one encore to play before the show ended. They then had a meet and greet before heading back to the hotel for a late dinner.

Cal ran his eyes down the long checklist of things he needed to do for the meet and greet. As soon as the guys finished on stage, he'd head up to the reception room that had been reserved for them. He'd prepped the room earlier with photographs for the band to sign and ensured that there were plenty of Sharpies available.

He returned his attention to the stage to catch the last few moments of the show. He tried not to let all of his focus land on Seth, but it was difficult. The man really did know how to work a stage and the crowd. With a final, lingering glance, Cal headed backstage to make sure everything was ready for the meet and greet.

Two hours later, Cal watched as Sarge expertly herded the stragglers out of the reception room where the meet and greet had been held. Cal started packing away the surplus photos and posters and picking up the pens the guys had used. He'd started out watching quietly from the corner but had soon been roped into snapping pictures of fans with the band. He was now very familiar with the idiosyncrasies of most models of smartphones.

"Thanks for your help today, Cal."

Cal, startled at the sound of Seth's voice and turned to face the guitarist. He noticed the fine lines of tiredness around the dark eyes and gave Seth a gentle smile.

"You're welcome, but you don't have to thank me for doing my job."

"Yeah, we do. We couldn't do what we do if it wasn't for people like you behind the scenes." Seth gave him a quizzical look and Cal guessed the surprise he was feeling was probably showing on his face.

"Don't tell me no one's ever thanked you before," he was asked.

"Well, um, no, not really," Cal said, rubbing a hand self-consciously through his hair. He'd always been a "behind the scenes" guy, and he knew Jax appreciated his help, but he'd never expected the band to really notice what he was doing.

"Well, whoever your previous employers were, they suck," Seth declared.

"You've got that right," Cal muttered without thinking. Systems Corp still hadn't paid him the money they owed him, and he was starting to worry about how he would make his next student loan payment.

"Hey, Cal, ready to go?" Sarge called across the room.

"Yeah," Cal confirmed, closing the lid on the last storage box. He smiled at Seth. "By the way, great show tonight. I really enjoyed it."

"Thanks. The first show is always a test, but there weren't too many problems. We'll go over them with Larry tomorrow before the next show."

Seth looked like he wanted to say more, but a not-so-discrete cough from Sarge stopped him. He shoved his hands in the pockets of his leather jacket and gave Cal a nod.

"See you later, at dinner?"

"Yeah, I'm nearly done here. See you there."

Seth strode out of the room and Cal tried to ignore the frown on his cousin's face.

"Don't go there, Cal," warned Sarge.

Irritation flashed through Cal, but he tried not to let it show. "Go where? I'm just doing my job."

"Look, Seth is a nice guy. In private, he's very different to the persona he puts out there to the public, but, and I say this with nothing but love and concern for you, Cal, he's not relationship material, and I'd hate to see you hurt."

"First, who said anything about a relationship?" Cal fired at his cousin. "And, second, *if* I did want to go there, it would be none of your business. I'm a grown man, capable of making my own decisions. I'm aware that Seth has a reputation, but honestly, he wouldn't look at me that way even if I wanted him to."

Sarge huffed grumpily next to him as they made their way down the stairs to the exit. "Cal, you've had a hell of a few months. I don't want to see you get dealt another blow on top of what has already happened."

"Ugh, I know, Sarge, and I'll never be able to repay you and Jax back for everything you've done for me. But I can look after myself."

"You don't have to pay us back, and I don't care how old you are. You'll always be my baby cousin, and I'll always look out for you."

Cal rolled his eyes and shoved at Sarge's meaty shoulder. "Go look out for those you're paid to look out for."

Sarge gave him an affectionate smile before heading over to where the band was waiting. After a brief consultation with the others on the security team, Cal watched him usher the laughing bandmates out of the door.

***

Seth sauntered over to where Liam and Jamie were sitting, their heads close together as they talked. From the way their eyes kept darting to where Kellet was sitting with his family, Seth could figure out the topic of their conversation.

"I think he'll be okay," he heard Jamie say, and Liam chuckled next to him.

"Just for the record, I'm more than happy to be the go-to guy for calming nerves before a show. However, you're the only one that can sort out the unresolved sexual tension between the two of you," Liam retorted, nudging his shoulder against Jamie's.

"Yes, for fuck's sake, can you two screw each other's brains out already," Seth said, slinging an arm around each of their shoulders as he leaned between them.

"Really, Seth?" Jamie said, with a glare. "Look, we're going at his pace. I'm not going to lose him again, guys."

"Maybe I should give him a nudge in the right direction then," Seth declared, standing up straight as though to confront Kellet. It had the desired effect as Jamie grabbed his wrist before he could move.

"Seth," Jamie growled. "Leave it!"

"Jay, it's as plain as day that he wants you as much as you want him. I thought you two would have gotten down to it already."

"It's not that simple, Seth. I don't need you sticking your nose in where it's not needed," Jamie snapped back, making Seth realize maybe Jamie wasn't as relaxed as he was trying to appear about the lack of action between him and their drummer.

"Okay, both of you just chill," Liam said, ever the peacemaker. "Seth, it's Jamie and Kel's business, and you need to stay out of it."

"Yeah, it's not like we're mentioning anything about you and Cal," Jamie said with a smirk. Seth gaped at him.

"Whadda mean? Me and Cal? Nothing going on. F'r fuck's sake, he's the *intern*," Seth said the last word with a hiss.

"I've seen the way you look at him. You can pretend that you won't go near him because he's part of the team, and for all your other fucked up morals, you do actually respect the golden rule of not screwing the crew. I'm just sayin', if he *wasn't* staff, then you'd be all over him like a rash."

Liam chuckled and held out a fist to Jamie, who grinned as they bumped knuckles.

"Don't forget. Being Sarge's cousin also adds another layer of 'do not touch' to the whole scenario," Liam commented, winking at Jamie as he finished his beer.

"Assholes. That's what you both are," Seth declared with a huff. "I'm leaving now before someone gets offended. I'll see you later."

Stalking from the restaurant, Seth tried to suppress the feelings of hurt and anger Jamie's words had invoked. He hadn't realized that his attraction to Cal had been so obvious, but Jamie was right, he wouldn't act on it. Seth knew it wasn't fair to Cal, and from his interactions with him, Seth knew Cal wasn't one-night stand material. He had relationship written all over him. Not that that was a bad thing, Seth wasn't relationship adverse, but he'd seen too many crash and burn to want to partake himself.

Unless you find someone willing to put up with the nomadic lifestyle. Seth groaned at himself. He was willing to admit he was jealous of Jamie and Kellet and the relationship they were slowly forging. But it would work for them, as they were both living the same lifestyle. Asking anyone to put up with him being away for two-thirds of a year was asking a lot.

Sure, his partner could travel with them, but he didn't want someone who didn't have their own life and dreams. He wanted someone independent but also someone that loved him for him. Warts and all. Maybe, after the tour, he should look at trying to find a serious relationship. Besides, if he was to honor the stupid condition his aunt had put in her will, he did need to find a partner sooner rather than later.

Really, who in this day and age put a stipulation on a bequest that the beneficiary had to be married for a year before they could receive the money. It's not like he needed the money, but the other kicker was that if he didn't meet the requirements, then the money passed to his aunt's brother, his father. And there was no way in hell he was letting his parents get one cent of his aunt's money.

They didn't deserve one red cent, something his aunt knew. They both came from moderate, upper-middle-class backgrounds and there was no denying his father had worked hard for the money he had now. But, as their fortunes had grown, his parents had taken on the airs and graces of the nouveau riche and looked down on anyone they considered less than them.

His aunt Rosemary had married very well but had never forgotten her roots, donating her time and money to various causes. Her untimely passing nearly three years ago from breast cancer had left a huge hole in Seth's life. She had always supported his music and art endeavors when his own parents had all but disowned him when he'd refused to go to college and get a degree in law, medicine, or business; the three acceptable areas of study for a son of Donald and Elaine Worthington.

His parents had pandered to his music choices when he was in high school, and when Miles had turned up with a contract just as they were graduating, Seth had jumped at the chance to follow his dreams. It had been Aunt Rosemary who had stood by him and convinced his parents that he was young enough that if things didn't work out with Larkspur, he could get an appropriate degree then.

Seventeen years later, he had more money and success than his parents, brother, and aunt put together. However, his parents still thought he had wasted his life and, even as recently as last Christmas, had asked if he was ever going to settle down and do something meaningful. It never ceased to amaze Seth that they hadn't latched onto his success, using it to get ahead in social circles. The parents of his bandmates certainly bragged about their sons and how proud they were. But then again, they also didn't use those bragging rights to make themselves look better than anyone else. And neither did his parents. They bragged about how successful Art was and how well his small law firm was growing, but because being a musician didn't rate as a 'proper job', Seth's many accomplishments were not discussed.

He stabbed at the elevator button as he muttered and cursed under his breath. He'd have to apologize to his friends in the morning. Seth knew he was being an asshole, and he was glad his best friends wouldn't take it personally.

The doors to the elevator finally opened, and he stepped into the empty car. He sighed in relief as the doors began to close. He really didn't want to deal with anyone right now.

"Hold the door!"

Seth jerked in surprise at the shout and instinctively pressed the button on the panel. His heart lurched when Cal grinned at him and slid through the gap.

"Thanks, Seth."

"You're welcome," Seth replied, tension releasing from his shoulders as Cal settled in beside him. A faint scent of sunshine and lemons had Seth wondering what cologne Cal used. "What floor?" he asked, nodding at the panel.

"Oh, twentieth, same as you guys."

"Not slumming it with the crew on the sixth floor, then?"

Cal shook his head. "No. One perk of the job. Jax booked me onto your floor, so I'm around if she needs me for anything."

"Makes sense," Seth agreed, resting his shoulder into the corner, trying to appear nonchalant as all his senses clamored to tug Cal close and bury his face in the smooth nape of his neck.

A few moments later, the elevator slid to a smooth stop, and with a ding, the doors opened. Seth waved Cal through first, his eyes dropping to Cal's tight backside. He mentally slapped himself and glanced up just in time as Cal turned to face him.

"So, I'm down this way in 2010," he said, nodding down the corridor.

"I'm in 2018," Seth replied, and together they walked down the corridor.

"I suppose this is all old hat to you," Cal said.

"Yeah, we've stayed here for the last few years every time we're in New York."

"Do you still enjoy all the traveling?"

"Yes and no," Seth admitted and caught a surprised look on Cal's face. "I mean, I love playing and sharing our music with the fans. There's really nothing like it when you're out there on that stage. But the constant moving from city to city, living out of a suitcase for months on end; yeah, that bit soon gets old."

"Huh, true. Hadn't really thought about it like that," Cal mused as his step slowed. He nodded at the room they were in front of. "This is me," he said, but made no move to open the door.

"Thanks again for your help today," Seth told him, tucking his hands into his leather jacket pockets.

Cal gave a small shrug. "Like I said, just doing my job."

"Are you enjoying it?" Seth asked, curious. He knew from various conversations that Cal's background was in IT. "It's not what you're used to doing."

"Yeah, I am. I mean, it's different from what I'm used to, but it's fun."

"I'm glad. I hope you know we appreciate your efforts."

Cal hitched his messenger bag on his shoulder, and his gaze didn't quite meet Seth's. "Thanks. That means a lot." His tongue flicked out, wetting his bottom lip. Seth's eyes were drawn to the movement. He took a half step forward, catching himself as Cal looked up. Their eyes met, and tension crackled between them.

"I should let you go," Seth told him, his voice husky.

"Yeah." Cal's voice was breathy. He reached into his jeans pocket, pulling out the key card. "Night, Seth."

"Night, Cal."

"See you in the morning. Breakfast meeting at eight," Cal reminded him as he turned away.

Seth nodded in acknowledgement as he headed to his room. "I'll be there."

The soft snick of Cal's door closing was the only response he got.

CHAPTER FIVE

*T*hree weeks later – Dallas

"*Sniper!*" The yell from Sarge had Seth cramming himself further into the dark corner he had taken refuge in. He carefully scanned his immediate area, trying to spot where the shot had come from, but there were too many flashes in the dim light from the other laser guns for him to figure it out.

He spotted Sarge a few feet away, the former ex-Marine stalking slowly through the maze, his plastic gun held at eye level as he tried to find out where the sniper was. A shot fired from somewhere above Seth and Sarge's vest flashed from blue to red, showing he'd been hit.

"Damn it, Callahan. Wait until I get my hands on you!" Sarge roared, his head twisting left and right as he searched out his attacker.

Liam scurried past them and patted Sarge on the shoulder sympathetically. "You shouldn't have taught him so well," he said before disappearing into the depths of the warehouse they were in.

"I should have known better than to let the roadies grab him for their team," Sarge muttered as he tucked in beside Seth.

"Do you think we can make it to the next corner?" Seth asked, nodding towards the next set of obstacles.

"We can try," Sarge confirmed as his vest recharged and changed back to blue, indicating he was live again. "You go first, and I'll cover your six."

Seth nodded and dashed away, Sarge hot on his heels. He swung behind the inflated wall and crashed into two other people, their vests dark.

"Ow, fuck! Watch it, Seth," Jamie grumbled as Seth steadied them both.

"You okay, JJ?" Kellet asked, concern in his tone.

"I'm fine, Kel," Jamie reassured his boyfriend.

"Ugh, don't tell me you two are finding dark corners to make out in?" Seth moaned.

"Alright, we won't," Jamie replied with a chuckle.

"Jay, you can do that when we get back to the hotel. Right now, we've got to capture the flag and reclaim our crown from the crew. I won't allow them to beat us two tours in a row."

"Good luck with that," Kellet said dryly. "I saw Wil, Sam, and Cal strategizing earlier. We haven't got a hope of winning. Do you know how many hours those three have spent playing video games? And add in Cal's skills as a developer, they could beat us with their eyes closed and one hand tied behind their backs."

"Cal could do it single-handedly. Kid's been shooting since he was big enough to hold a rifle," Sarge told them before sticking his head out and shooting at a hapless crew member who wandered too close.

"Wait, you're talking about assistant Cal?" Seth asked, tugging on the back of Sarge's vest. "Small, blond, twink-looking? Won't say boo to a goose and looks scared to death every time I talk to him? That Cal?"

Sarge sighed as he turned to look at Seth. "Yes. My cousin, Callahan Stevens. He's a crack shot. Junior state champion. And don't let him hear you calling him a twink, or you'll be next in his sights." Sarge nodded towards the maze. "We need to get out there. We're gonna lose if we don't make a run for the flag."

He pointed at Kellet and Jamie. "You two break left, Seth and I'll break right." At their nods, he took a breath and lifted a fist with three fingers raised. He slowly lowered each one and then took off, Seth following him closely.

A second later, there was a flash of light, and Seth's vest vibrated. "Ah, fuck! I've been hit," he yelled as he dived for cover next to Sarge.

"Doesn't matter, we're too late," Sarge said, waving a hand towards the center cage where Wil was doing a victory dance with a large red flag, and a siren sounded, signaling the end of the game.

Seth stood, brushed himself down, and noticed movement out of the corner of his eye. He swung round to see a grinning Cal slither down from a hidden perch just above where they'd been hiding.

Cal casually slung his laser rifle onto his shoulder and walked towards them with a swagger so sexy and confident, Seth was sure it couldn't be the same young man who had been on tour with them for the last few weeks.

"So that's where you were hiding," Sarge said, grinning at his cousin. "How'd you know it was there?"

"I got a tour when I came to confirm the booking for Jax," Cal replied smugly. "I managed to sneak up on it when you were all getting the safety briefing."

"That's... that's cheating!" Seth spluttered. "We should win by default. You guys had an unfair advantage."

"All's fair in love and war," Cal said, leaning up to pat Seth on the cheek. "At least, that's what Sarge always told me."

Seth froze at the contact as heat shot through him. Who was this man? Cal had been slowly losing his quiet reserve around them—well, Seth at least, he didn't have the same issues around any of the others—and now he was standing in front of Seth like he owned the world, and he knew it.

Seth's gaze ran down the man in front of him. Cal's fine features were suffused with a glow, happiness and excitement shining in his eyes, a bright grin in place of the usual shy smile. It was all Seth could do to stop himself from kissing the man senseless right where they stood.

His eyes returned to Cal's face, and the other man was once again blushing under the scrutiny, his air of bravado fading.

"Cal, come on," Wil called. "We've got to get our trophy."

"Better not keep the kid waiting," Seth said, waving a hand to indicate that Cal should go first.

"Yeah, come on, Short Stuff, I owe you a beer after that performance," Sarge said, flinging his arm around Cal's shoulders and leading him away.

Seth watched them go and was surprised when Cal glanced back. Seth winked, and Cal stumbled before Sarge caught him and steered him towards the exit.

***

What the hell was I thinking, patting his cheek like that? Cal mentally kicked himself whilst trying to act unaffected by the memory of Seth's warm skin, roughened by the light stubble that shadowed the guitarist's firm jaw. *What would it feel like to have that scrape against his skin?*

"We did it, Cal!" Wil shouted, waving the red flag above his head. Cal was pulled from his thoughts as he was enveloped in an enthusiastic hug.

Cal laughed at the teenager's jubilation. Despite their age difference, they'd become good friends over the last couple of months.

"We sure did," he agreed.

"I still reckon you had an unfair advantage," Seth groused as he and the rest of the band joined them.

Cal blushed, something he still did around Seth, even though he was getting better at handling his attraction. He'd firmly placed Seth into the 'work colleague' category, and it was working, more or less. It was hard to ignore the man when he exuded sex, both on and off the stage. More than once, Cal had jerked off to images of Seth, hot and sweaty as he came offstage, eyes bright with adrenaline. They'd shared a few heated looks, but nothing more.

"Nah, you're just sore 'cos you old guys couldn't keep up with us young 'uns," Wil declared and then ducked away laughing as his father made a grab for him.

"Good shooting, Cal," Liam said, patting him on the shoulder.

"Thanks, Liam," Cal replied, smiling. He liked the bass guitarist, who was a little quieter and more unassuming than his bandmates. "You can thank Sarge, though. He taught me to shoot as a kid, and we still go out and practice whenever he's home."

Seth muttered under his breath but smirked at Cal when their glances caught, and Cal couldn't help the surge of heat that went through him. *Yep, it would be another long shower tonight.*

"Do we have time for a rematch?" Wil asked as they entered the waiting area, joining up with the rest of the crew.

Cal glanced at the large clock above the reception desk. Considering how quickly they had defeated the band, they probably could squeeze another quick round in. Cal looked at Sarge, who shrugged as if to say, *your call.*

"Does anyone else want another round?" he asked, and there were affirmatives from all sides of the room. Cal nodded and was about to check with the staff if they could go another round when Seth's voice stopped him.

"Only if we change the teams around."

"No! Same teams, or it means the crew keeps the cup by default," Wil shot back.

"He's right," Jamie said as Seth looked ready to argue the point. Holding up a placating hand to his bandmate, he continued, "but Cal has to give us five minutes before he enters the game to even up the odds a little."

"How is that fair? You've got Sarge. He's just as good as Cal is," Wil argued back.

Before the issue could devolve into a major argument, Cal stepped in. "I agree."

"But...."

"Don't worry, Wil, we'll still beat them," he said, with a confidence he didn't really have.

Wil nodded his head but didn't look happy.

Cal made his way over to the desk and a few minutes later, he stood and watched as everyone disappeared back into the gaming area.

The young staff member started the game and then a countdown clock. Cal watched on the screens placed around the waiting area, laughing as crew and band alike scattered like rats in a maze, heading as far in as they could to try to reach the flag first. He tried to keep track of Seth but lost him after a few seconds.

His time penalty was soon up, and sliding his weapon into place, Cal cautiously stepped into the darkened area. He wasn't naïve enough to imagine that someone wouldn't be waiting to ambush him and keep him out of the game as long as possible.

He slid left, scanning the area in front of him. He needed to get to the flag area on the opposite side of the warehouse. Keeping as tight to the wall as possible, he inched along, searching for anyone stalking him. He came to a junction, and he knew he had to make a break across the open area to get to the next bit of cover. He checked his gun was fully primed and eased his finger onto the trigger. It certainly wasn't as sensitive as the trigger on his .308 hunting rifle, which only needed a gentle twitch of his finger to fire. This lump of molded plastic wasn't bad for the job it was designed for, but it certainly took more effort than a real firearm.

He gave a last glance before taking a breath, preparing to dart across the gap, when a warm hand gripped his bicep and tugged him around the corner. A startled yelp escaped him, and he just prevented himself from swinging the laser gun at the assailant's head when he realized he was staring into Seth's grinning face.

"Gotchya!"

"Jesus fucking Christ, Seth!" The words fell from his mouth, and the stunned look on Seth's face was priceless at the unexpected profanity. "What the hell are you doing?"

"I'm kidnapping you to stop you from getting that flag," Seth told him with a wicked grin.

"You could have just shot me," Cal exclaimed, waving a hand at his vest.

"But where's the fun in that?"

When Cal just stared at him, the humor in Seth's face faded to be replaced by concern.

"I didn't hurt you, did I?" he asked, rubbing a gentle hand over Cal's bicep, causing tingles to chase down his spine.

"What... um, no. No, just surprised me, that's all," Cal replied, willing his heartbeat to slow down and his cock to stop thickening.

He felt the brush of Seth's thumb against his throat, and he swallowed deeply.

"Your pulse is racing," Seth said quietly as he stroked against Cal's heated flesh. "Did I really scare you that much, or..." Seth paused, his head tilting as his gaze became hooded. "Or is your heart racing for another reason?"

Cal licked his suddenly dry lips, and Seth's eyes followed the movement.

"Oh, fuck it!" Seth growled before stepping closer as he tilted Cal's head back. Cal had less than a second to realize what was about to happen before a warm mouth landed on his. His brain went offline, and without thought, his eyes fluttered closed as he parted his lips as Seth's tongue flickered against them.

Cal lost all thought as Seth's tongue plundered his mouth. He tasted the hint of mint from the gum Seth had been chewing earlier, and being this close, the scent of warm male enveloped Cal. His fingers brushed against the stud in Seth's ear as his hand crept around Seth's neck. His fingers tangled in the hair at the nape of Seth's neck, the strands silky soft. The faint scratch of Seth's stubble abraded his skin, and Cal wanted to feel more of it across the rest of his body.

Their bulky vests prevented them from getting closer, and Cal moaned softly in protest. Seth slowed the kiss, pulling away with several lingering pecks. He brushed his thumb over Cal's cheek, and Cal reluctantly opened his eyes. He was met with a heated dark glaze, Seth's pupils blown. They both were panting, and Cal reluctantly let go, his mind racing.

"I'd apologize, but—"

"No apology needed," Cal broke in, his voice cracking. He cleared his throat, stepping away from the heat of Seth's body. He nodded towards the gaming area. "We should really...."

Seth's gaze searched his face, and Cal was aware that his elbow was still held in a light grip. "Yeah, we should," Seth agreed. "You... ah, you go first. I'll give you a few seconds head start."

Before he could second guess himself, Cal popped up on his toes and pressed a brief kiss to Seth's mouth. "May the odds be ever in your favor." He winked at a stunned Seth and dashed out into the maze.

Ducking around a corner, he paused to catch his breath. *Seth kissed me!* He really didn't know what to make of it. He'd never thought Seth would act on his attraction to Cal. The sound of a vest beeping nearby pulled him from his thoughts. He could revisit them later, in the privacy of his hotel shower. With a grin, he dived into the darkness. He had a flag to win.

CHAPTER SIX

C al stood at the entrance to the conference hall which was teeming with people attending the huge tech conference in Las Vegas. He hadn't seen anyone he knew but wouldn't be surprised if someone from his old life was there.

He wasn't an official attendee, so he only observed as harried-looking interns raced around hawking their CV's to equally harried looking lower management executives in between promoting and pushing whatever project they were currently working on.

He was hoping to run into a familiar face so he could pass on his own resume, but he wasn't really sure if he wanted to return to the stress and uncertainty of gaming and app development. He'd enjoyed the change of pace being on tour with Larkspur, but it didn't pay enough, and while the work was fun, it wasn't challenging enough for him in the long term.

A reminder buzzed on his phone, and with a sigh, he made his way to the lobby where the band was meeting to head back to the arena for the second sold out show. Tomorrow they would travel to Denver for one more concert, then they had eight days off before regrouping in Seattle to finish out the last few weeks of the tour.

After tonight's show, he'd head to one of the numerous hotel bars to see if he could connect with any of the vendors who would be busy networking.

Slipping his tablet from his messenger bag, he brought up the checklist for tonight's show. A quick glance through saw that everything was on schedule and as long as they didn't get caught in traffic, they should make the sound check with time to spare.

A message flashed across the screen from Sarge to say the band was on their way down. Cal moved outside into the sticky heat and slipped into the rear seat of one of the waiting SUVs. He'd learned very quickly to be in place before Larkspur appeared so as not to get lost in the melee of fans.

He was updating his to-do list and wishing for the hundredth time that it would automatically update Jax's, but the software was too old. The SUV rocked gently as a body climbed in, and he spared a quick glance to see who it was. When his eyes met Seth's twinkling blue eyes, his stomach lurched before settling. *Would there ever be a time he didn't react to Seth?* Since their kiss last week, it had been harder to keep his emotions and desire in check. Neither of them had mentioned it, but Cal wasn't sure if anyone else on the tour had picked up on their heated glances and overly polite conversations.

"Hey, Cal. All good to go?"

"Hmm, oh, yeah. Everything is on schedule," he confirmed back. The SUV rocked again as Liam slid in next to Seth.

Cal frowned as the bass player settled into his seat. "Aren't you supposed to be with Jamie, and Kellet in with us?"

"I tried, but those two are joined at the hip," Liam muttered. "It was just easier to jump in here than make a scene where everyone and their phone can see."

"Fair enough," Cal agreed and then returned his attention to his tablet, keenly aware of Seth's broad shoulders in the seat in front of him. His fingers itched as he remembered the feel of the closely shaved hair that tapered into the nape of his neck.

Tonight, as like every other night they performed, Seth's faux hawk stood tall. The shaved sides looked freshly done, and Cal resisted the urge to lean forward and press his mouth to the warm skin.

As though he could feel Cal's gaze, Seth twisted in his seat and glanced over his shoulder. Cal darted his eyes back to his tablet, but from the soft chuckle, he knew he hadn't fooled Seth.

A notification flashed in the corner of his tablet from his personal email. His stomach lurched when he recognized the sender as the finance company he had his loan with. Swallowing, he opened the email, the feeling of nausea deepening as he read another warning regarding his payments. He really needed to call and talk to someone about his situation, as his emails were obviously being disregarded, just like the ones to Systems Corp about his payout. He knew that his former employers had a booth at the convention, but getting to see them would be difficult and there wouldn't be anyone there that would have any influence to look into why he hadn't been paid yet. Anger and frustration warred through him. He just wanted the whole sorry mess dealt with. He must have made a sound because Seth turned and looked at him with a frown.

"Everything okay, Cal?"

"Yeah," Cal nodded with a smile that he hoped was reassuring, but from the way Seth's frown deepened, he had failed.

"You sure?"

"Yep, all good. Just a couple of details I need to sort out. Nothing that is going to affect the show tonight."

Seth didn't look convinced, but to Cal's relief, he nodded and returned his attention to his phone.

Cal swiped out of his email and tried to get his thoughts back to the job at hand. He could sort the other out later.

Before long, they had reached the arena. Cal waited for Seth and Liam to exit, taking a moment to gather himself and allow the guys to get ahead. He tried to be as unobtrusive as possible because the fans could be overwhelming, and he didn't need that kind of attention in his life. With a final check to make sure his credentials were in place around his neck, he slipped from the car and crossed to the entry. With a nod and wave to one of Sarge's team on the door, he slid into the cool backstage area of the arena and headed towards command central, where Jax was waiting for him.

***

Seth handed his guitar off to Blue in exchange for a bottle of water and towel with a grin and a nod of thanks. Another show down, and it had been another sellout performance. The fans had been buzzing, and Seth was feeling on top of the world. After grabbing his bag from his dressing room, he made his way to the rear entrance to meet the others so they could head back to the hotel. He was too wired to hang in his room and was determined to convince his bandmates that they needed to go out for a drink or three.

He reached the meeting point and was not surprised to find that Jamie and Kellet had yet to make an appearance. As he glanced round, he also noticed that Cal wasn't there either, which was unusual because he was usually waiting to go as soon as the band was. Seth's thoughts flicked back to the conversation on the way into the stadium. Cal had looked sick, and an overwhelming need to protect had swamped Seth. He was just about to ask Sarge where the younger man was when his missing bandmates appeared, hand in hand and looking decidedly rumpled.

"Glad you two decided to join us," Sarge grumbled. Seth laughed as both Jamie and Kellet shrugged and looked un-apologetic for holding them up. Sarge muttered into the comms device, checking with Ross, one of the other security team to ensure the car was ready, and then followed the big man outside. There were some lingering fans, and Seth grinned and waved before clambering into the limo waiting for them.

"Great show tonight, guys," he congratulated his bandmates as he settled into his seat.

"Yeah, it went off really well. The crowd was amazing," Jamie agreed as he snuggled into Kellet's side.

"I suppose you two are going to disappear as soon as we get back to the hotel?"

Jamie nodded as he gave Kellet a heated look and Seth knocked his foot against Jamie's. "Oi, less of the eye-fucking, please."

The two men grinned at him and got even closer. Seth rolled his eyes at their antics and nudged Liam. "You'll come out for a drink with me, won't you, Lee?"

"Huh? Oh, yeah, I suppose so," Liam replied, barely looking up from his phone.

"What's got you so distracted?" Seth asked, leaning over to see Liam's phone.

"Nothing, just checking the comments from tonight's show."

"Anything we should be worried about?" Kellet asked.

"Nah, all very positive," Liam reassured him. "I need to do a proper analysis, but it looks like we're ahead of budget for this stage of the tour," he added, slipping into his unofficial manager role.

"That definitely deserves a drink," Seth declared as he fixed his gaze on Jamie. "Come on, you two. Come out for just a couple of drinks and then you can go and fuck each other into oblivion."

Jamie glanced at Kellet before sighing and nodding slowly. "Two drinks only, but you have to give us half an hour at the hotel to shower and change."

"Uh huh, as long as it is only thirty minutes," Seth agreed. "If you're not in the bar after that, I'll publish your room number on Twitter."

Jamie rolled his eyes but nodded his agreement. Seth nudged Liam's shoulder. "You as well."

"Okay."

"Wow, once more with less enthusiasm, Lee," Seth replied to his bandmate's lackluster response.

Liam grunted and returned his attention to his phone. Seth threw a questioning look at Jamie and Kellet, both of whom looked as mystified as he was. Yeah, sure, Liam was the quietest of the four of them. Had always been a bit more serious, but even he'd been quieter than usual this tour.

"Hey, you okay?" Seth asked him quietly. "If you really don't want to come out, that's fine."

"What?" Liam flicked a glance at Seth and then seemed to gather himself. "Yeah, I'm good. Just tired, that's all. You know how it gets at this stage of the tour."

"Yeah, I know. We haven't played for so many weeks without a break for years. I'm still not sure why management scheduled our break so late in the tour."

"Oh, it was due to booking conflicts with another couple of bands. It was the only way we could play the venues we wanted," Liam explained. Seth nodded, remembering vaguely the issue being discussed, but to be honest, he rarely took note of the details. Even though Miles was their manager, Liam had always looked out for them that way,. Liam had been their unofficial manager when they started out and had continued to keep an eye on their contracts, sales, and social media presence. This wasn't because they didn't trust Miles—he was one of the rare, good ones in the industry who stood by clients and took their wants and wishes into consideration—but Liam was a control freak, and he and Miles had worked out a good working relationship.

"Only a few more days then, and we're home for a break. Got anything planned?" Seth asked. "I mean, we know what these two are going to be up to," he said with a nod at the couple seated across from him, to which Kellet responded with a finger which had them all laughing.

"Just going to chill around home," Liam said. "What about you?"

"About the same. Going to catch up with Art, but no other plans."

"What, no parade of fuck buddies lined up?" Liam teased. "I have to say I'm surprised. You've been remarkably restrained this leg of the tour, or have you been so discreet that we haven't noticed?"

"Yeah, what's that all about, Seth? You usually have some groupie hanging off your dick," Jamie said.

"I... I just haven't had the urge this tour," Seth replied, trying to throw them off, but realizing that it was actually the truth. *Huh, what was up with that?*

"Hmm, I wonder why?" Kellet asked, grinning.

Jamie gave a mock gasp and clutched a hand to his chest. "Do you think a certain blond assistant may have something to do with it?"

"What? No! Fuck's sake, guys." Even to his own ears, Seth's protests sounded weak.

"We've seen how you look at him, Seth," Liam chimed in. "You can try to deny it all you like, but you're lusting after Cal. I'm surprised you haven't made a move yet."

Seth struggled to find a reply that didn't incriminate him. However, his silence must have been telling because Jamie sat up straight and pinned him with a wide-eyed gaze.

"Oh my God! Have you slept with Cal? What happened to not screwing the crew, Seth?"

"No! I haven't slept with him. For fuck's sake, give me some credit."

All three men snorted their amusement, and Seth flipped them all off.

"I'm just not interested in playing the field, alright? I mean, seeing you two finally get your shit together has made me realize maybe it would be nice to have that one person."

"Aww, our little Seth is growing up," Jamie said, wiping an imaginary tear from his eye, before slyly adding, "and you'd like that one person to be Cal?"

"Fuck off, Jay," Seth retorted, causing another round of laughter. "Cal's a good guy. Too good for me."

There were general comments of agreement all round, and the teasing continued until they pulled up in front of the hotel. As they prepared to get out, Seth pulled out his phone and made a show of setting the timer and waving it in Jamie and Kellet's faces.

"Thirty minutes and not a second longer!"

CHAPTER SEVEN

S eth relaxed back in the booth he had commandeered and grinned as he spotted Jamie and Kellet winding their way through the crowd. Fingers entwined and as little space between them as possible. As they shuffled their way into seats, Seth glanced at the non-existent watch on his wrist and complimented them on their time keeping.

Jamie huffed a reply before grabbing one of the bottles of beer Liam pushed towards him.

"Sure is packed in here tonight," Kellet remarked as he looked around.

Jamie nodded in agreement. "Yeah, apparently there's some tech show on?"

"It's the premier software developers' convention. The who's who of the software development world is here," Liam commented.

"And you know this how?" Jamie drawled, beating Seth to the question.

"Cal mentioned it when we were in Houston."

Sarge, who was keeping watch and deterring any over-enthusiastic fans from approaching, whipped his head around at

Liam's comments. "Damn, I'd forgotten about that," he said as he pulled out his phone.

"Everything okay, Sarge?" Kellet asked their burly body-guard, who was now scanning the bar with a worried frown.

"What? Oh, yeah, fine," he replied distractedly. "Hey, will you guys be okay for a few minutes? I need to check in with Cal."

"Of course," Jamie reassured him. "What's up with Cal? Is there anything we can do?"

"It's not my story to tell, but let's just say that there are some real sharks in the IT world, and Cal got caught up in some shit that went down," Sarge said.

"Sarge, go find him. We're not going to be here for much longer. I'm sure we can manage to stay out of trouble," Jamie said.

"I've got hold of Ross. He'll be here in five minutes," Sarge told them, naming one of the other bodyguards on the team.

"Go, Sarge," Seth said, waving a hand at the bigger man who was visibly concerned. An itch settled at the back of Seth's neck, and he began scanning the crowd. His eyes snagged on several blond heads, but none were Cal, and the thought of sitting and drinking with his friends lost its appeal, and all he wanted to do was go and find the missing man. Ever since their stolen kiss in Dallas, he'd had to work extra hard to stay away from the enticing blond, and his sketchbook was filled with images of Cal.

Draining the bottle of beer in his hand, he continued to search the crowd, his eyes flicking past those of people obviously wanting to make eye contact. Past Seth would have jumped at the opportunity, but tonight—in fact, this whole leg of the tour, as his bandmates had so kindly pointed out—he wasn't interested.

He noticed Kellet and Jamie whispering to each other and was about to give them shit for it when his gaze snagged on another blond head. A surge of familiarity went through him at the sight.

"There he is," he said, moving to his feet before his brain had even caught up with the action.

"Who?" Liam asked, looking in the direction Seth was staring.

"Cal. I'm going to go and see if he's okay," he said, sliding out of the booth.

"Good. I'll message Sarge and let him know where he is," Liam said.

"We're heading out," Jamie said, standing up and tugging Kellet's hand so the other man could slide out behind him.

"Yeah. Cool. See ya in the morning," Seth replied distractedly, missing the looks his bandmates threw at him.

Shoving his phone into the pocket of his short leather jacket, he made his way towards Cal. The guy looked despondent, and Seth wanted to wrap him in his arms and solve all his problems.

A tug on his sleeve had him stopping, and he found himself face-to-face with a young man. Seth looked at him and then down at the hand on his arm.

"Hi," the young man said with a flirty grin. "You're Seth from Larkspur, aren't you?"

Groaning internally, Seth plastered on his "meeting-the-public" smile. He really didn't have the time or inclination to do this now.

"Yes, I am."

"I thought so. I just wanted to say hi and tell you how much I loved the show tonight." The hand on his sleeve crept up towards Seth's bicep.

"I'm glad you enjoyed it."

"Could I, perhaps, buy you a drink?"

Seth gently removed the hand that had somehow migrated to the lapel of his jacket. "That's really kind of you, but I'm meeting a friend, and I'm already late."

Disappointment flashed across the young man's face, but he took the rebuff at face value and stepped away. "Oh, okay, thanks. I hope you have a good night."

"Thanks, you too."

Seth gave him a more natural smile before turning back to make sure Cal hadn't moved. Relief flooded him when he saw Cal was still at the table at the end of the bar. Deciding he needed a drink, Seth changed trajectory and headed towards the bar. He caught the bartender's attention and ordered two beers. Within moments, he was served. With a nod of thanks and a generous tip, he started to make his way over to Cal.

As he drew closer, he spotted two suit-clad men approach Cal and Seth paused to watch. Something about their demeanor and the way Cal had stiffened when he'd noticed them had all of Seth's senses on alert. Something wasn't quite right. Cal hadn't noticed Seth, all his attention was on the two men in front of him. Seth was close enough to eavesdrop on their conversation despite the crowd talking and laughing around him.

"Cal, old buddy. Didn't think we'd see you here," the taller of the two men said. His tone was overly jovial and insincere.

"Oh, hey Clive," Cal said before nodding at the other man. "Beck."

"Cal, how've you been? Who are you here with?" the man called Beck asked.

"Oh, I'm not here for the conference," Cal replied, and Seth noticed how his shoulders tensed even further.

"Here for pleasure, then? Spending up some of the settlement you got, eh? Good on you."

A flash of what looked like pain crossed Cal's features, and Seth took another step closer.

"You guys here with Systems Corp?"

"Yeah. We're ah... scouting for some new interns. You know how it is, always got to keep the blood fresh, keep the ideas new and current."

Cal hunched in further on himself; before Seth could stop himself, he was next to Cal in a few short strides.

"Here you go, babe. Sorry it took so long. Got caught up with a fan," he said, placing the drink on the table. Cal's wide green eyes flew to his face, and Seth saw the brief flash of confusion before relief flooded his features.

"Th...thanks."

Seth gave him a soft smile before turning to the two men looking at him in confusion. Never let it be said that the media training drilled into them from day one had been ignored. Switching on his best public smile, Seth stuck out a hand.

"Hi, I'm Seth."

"Hi. I'm Clive, and this is Beck," the taller of the two replied, giving Seth's hand a curt shake.

"Sorry, where are my manners," Cal said, and Seth was relieved to see some of the tension had left his body. "Clive, Beck, and I used to work together."

"And how do you two know each other?" Clive asked. "You're from that band, aren't you?"

"Yeah, I'm the lead guitarist for Larkspur," Seth replied, not liking Clive's tone.

"I'm working with the band while they're on tour," Cal said quietly.

Incredulous looks crossed both men's faces. "Working for a band? Why aren't you with one of the big software firms?" Beck asked, confused.

"I needed a change of scenery, and this opportunity came up. I'll look for something else once the tour is over," Cal replied, stiffening beside Seth. Seth's instincts prickled. Cal wasn't lying exactly, but he also wasn't telling the whole truth.

"So, you two are...." Clive asked, glancing between the two of them.

The insinuation had all of Seth's protective instincts firing. Without a second thought, he slipped an arm across Cal's shoulders and pulled him close to his body. He felt Cal's breath hitch and prayed the younger man would play along.

"Um... er... yeah. We're—" Cal looked blindly at Seth for help.

"You don't sound so sure, Cal," Clive commented, and Seth decided he really didn't like this person.

"Not that it's any of your business, but we have to be discreet, y'know, seeing as I'm a fairly public figure." Seth slipped a bit of the Worthington family arrogance into his tone, and a small thrill of pleasure went through him as Clive took a step back.

"Of course, I didn't mean to imply otherwise," came the flustered reply.

"So, hey, great to see you, Cal. When you're back home, give us a call, and we can grab a drink. Catch up properly," Beck said. "We need to go and check in with the guys. You take care now."

"Yeah. You too," Cal mumbled as the two men walked away.

Cal's shoulders slumped as soon as the men disappeared into the crowd, and Seth cupped the nape of Cal's neck and squeezed gently.

"What's going on, Cal?"

Cal startled, as though he'd forgotten Seth was there. "Oh, noth... nothing. Just some guys I use... used to work with."

"There's more than that. Come on, Cal. You can talk to me. I'd like to think we're friends."

"Fr... friends?"

"Yep. Look, why don't we get out of here? Find somewhere a bit quieter, and you can tell me the whole story." Cal looked like he was going to protest, but Seth pressed his finger to the soft lips. "Not taking no for an answer."

With a look of resignation, Cal nodded. Seth smiled and ran his thumb over Cal's mouth, resisting the urge to kiss him. The man looked like he could do with some loving and Seth wanted to be the man to do it.

He clasped Cal's hand in his, gently tugging him off the stool. "Come on, let's get out of here."

CHAPTER EIGHT

C al let himself be dragged across the crowded bar, the
warmth of Seth's calloused palm an anchor in a sea of
chaotic thoughts. Seth paused momentarily to glance at the
equally crowded lobby before turning on his heel and heading
in the opposite direction. Within moments, they were at the
entrance to a small lounge. Cal was vaguely aware of Seth talking
to the hostess before he was once again being led by Seth.

He distractedly took in the quiet ambiance of the lounge, a
small bubble of peace after the hubbub and noise of the main
bar area. A pianist played unobtrusively in the corner, and the
melodic tones settled Cal's nerves.

He'd felt sucker punched when Beck and Clive had appeared,
their demeanors grating on Cal's nerves. They obviously didn't
know that Cal hadn't been paid by Systems Corp, and the
ever-constant feeling of nausea had rolled through him at their
assumptions he was living the high life.

"Cal."

Seth's voice brought him back to himself, and he realized Seth
must have said his name more than once.

"Sorry, I zoned out there for a moment."

"That's okay," Seth said gently before nodding to the person standing next to their small table. "What would you like to drink?"

"Oh! Sorry, just a seltzer with a twist of lime, please."

The server smiled and left, leaving Cal and Seth alone. Cal looked around the room from the small private booth they were in. The dark leather was soft and welcoming, and Cal felt strangely safe. He finally let his gaze drift towards Seth and found himself being watched, and a flush warmed his face.

"Th... thanks for rescuing me."

"Anytime," Seth replied, resting his forearms on the table, leaning towards Cal. "You going to tell me who those clowns were and why you looked so sick when you were talking to them?"

He shook his head as shame flooded through him, and he dropped his gaze to the tabletop. He really didn't want to tell Seth what was going on. Hell, he'd barely been able to confide in Sarge and Jax, and he sure as hell didn't want to confide in the super-successful rock star in front of him.

"Hey, Cal. Look at me," Seth demanded, his tone gentle. "Whatever it is, we can work it out, okay."

"It's stupid," he whispered, causing Seth to shuffle closer to hear him.

"I'm sure it's not," Seth reassured him. "Besides, I'm the King of Stupid, so believe me, I doubt anything you could tell me would shock me."

Cal gave a small smile at the self-deprecating statement. Their server appeared with their drinks, and once they had gone, Cal took a sip of his drink as he gathered his thoughts. He was conscious of Seth waiting patiently beside him, sipping his whisky on the rocks.

"Like I said, I used to work with Clive and Beck. We've worked together since college when we were all interns at the same firm. Earlier this year, the company we worked for was bought out by a larger conglomerate, Systems Corp. They trimmed personnel, as they do when these takeovers happen, and I got let go, but they kept Clive and Beck on."

"That doesn't seem fair. Why did they keep those two and not you if you'd been a team for so long?"

"I don't know," Cal replied with a shrug.

"So why aren't you working for another tech company? Surely, with your experience, you'd be able to land a good role?"

Cal gave a bitter huff. "Yeah, you'd think so, wouldn't you? But somewhere along the line, I must have forgotten to make the appropriate sacrifice to whatever deity oversees computer geeks, 'cos, no one wanted me or my skills. I ran out of money and had to give up my apartment. Sarge and Jax rescued me, and Jax offered me the assistant job, and here we are." he finished with a flourish of hands like one of the dealers out on the gaming floor.

He braved a look at Seth and found the other man frowning at him. He replayed the words in his head, mentally groaning when he realized how ungrateful he sounded.

"Sorry, didn't mean to imply that working for you guys is a lesser job. It's not. I've loved every minute—"

"Cal, it's fine. I didn't think you meant that at all," Seth reassured him. "I'm just a bit confused. I didn't mean to eavesdrop earlier, but I thought I heard Clive mention a payout? Surely that would have been a fairly good amount?"

"It would have been if they'd actually paid it."

"What do you mean, 'if they'd paid it'?" Seth growled, his frown deepening.

Cal gave a helpless sigh and closed his eyes. He didn't want to see whatever look Seth was going to give him next.

"Exactly that. I've been chasing them for months, but they haven't replied to my emails or calls. I've used what little savings I had, and now the finance company that holds my student loan is chasing me for the payments I haven't been able to pay fully."

Despair washed through him, and he squeezed his eyes tighter to stop the tears he could feel building.

"Fuck, Cal! Why the hell haven't you said something? Surely Sarge would have helped you out."

He opened his eyes and stared at Seth helplessly. "I can't ask Sarge and Jax. I know they're comfortable, and they've already helped me by paying my outstanding utilities and back rent. What should I have said? *Thanks for helping me out, but do you have a spare sixty grand lying round I can borrow, y'know just till I get a real job and can spend the rest of my life paying you back?*""

Silence met his tirade, and Cal grew uncomfortable as Seth said nothing. A speculative look crossed his face, and his fingers began tapping out a beat on the tabletop.

"Why are you looking at me like that?" he asked warily.

Seth didn't reply, and nerves began to dance along Cal's spine. He didn't claim to know the man that well, but from what he observed over the last few months working with the band, this was Seth's dangerous face, and Cal was one hundred percent positive that he wasn't going to like what came out the sexy mouth.

"Marry me."

Cal blinked. Then he pinched himself. Did Seth just....

"Marry me, Cal."

Yep, he'd definitely just been proposed to. Sorta kinda.

CHAPTER NINE

S eth watched Cal pale and became concerned that the guy was going to pass out.

"Did... did you just pro... say marry you?"

Seth relaxed back into the soft leather of the club chair, stretching his long legs under the table, his foot grazing Cal's shin. He gave a slow nod and waited to see what Cal would say next.

"Wh... why? I mean..." Cal sighed, and the frown of confusion on his face deepened.

Seth took pity on the guy and leaned forward, resting his forearms on the table. He resisted taking one of Cal's hands into his, instead splaying his hands out. The light caught on one of the many rings that adorned most of his fingers.

"It's complicated, but basically, I need to get married."

"You need to get married?" Cal looked even more confused. "Why?"

"My aunt passed away nearly three years ago," Seth said, swallowing the lump in his throat that always hit when he thought about Rose Stanaway. "Anyway, she left me some money in her will. However, to inherit it I have to be married for a year, and the deadline to get married is creeping up."

"Huh?"

Seth grinned at Cal. "Yeah, I know. Very nineteenth century, but she had a wicked sense of humor, and it was her way of trying to get me to settle down."

"How much money are we talking about?"

"A hundred thousand dollars."

"A hundred thousand dollars? But, you make that in...." Cal tailed off as he realized what he said and his pale skin flushed red in embarrassment. "Sorry," he mumbled, dropping his gaze to the table.

Seth reached over and tilted Cal's face up, his thumb gently smoothing along Cal's jaw. The soft scrape of hidden stubble sending tingles up his arm.

"Hey, I know, okay. It's a ridiculous amount, and again, part of Aunt Rosie's humor."

"But why now? Why ask me to marry you?"

"She put a time limit on it. If I don't marry within three years of her death, the money will go to my father, her brother."

"And she died three years ago? So, the expiry date is coming up?"

Seth nodded. "Yep," he said, popping the 'p'.

"And you don't want your father to get the money?" Cal clarified.

"I don't want that bastard to get a red cent of it. Unfortunately, it looked like he was going to, but now, he won't. I'll marry you, get the money, and then, as your husband, gift it to you, and hey presto, your student loan is paid off, and we're both happy."

Cal blinked at him. Opened his mouth and closed it again. He reached for his drink, changed his mind and grabbed Seth's glass instead, and knocked back what was left of the whisky, coughing a little as the liquor hit the back of his throat. Seth glanced up and caught the eye of the server, signaling for two more whiskys.

"So, what do you think?" he asked when Cal didn't say anything, just staring at him.

"What do I think?" Cal flopped back into his chair and giggled. He leveled his gaze at Seth, and it took all Seth could do not to fall into the deep blue depths. "I think you're fucking crazy. That's what I think!"

***

Cal felt bad for the hurt look that flashed across Seth's face at his words, and with a groan, he closed his eyes and let his head fall backwards. He was vaguely aware of movement next to the table, and Seth's quiet thanks as their server placed two glasses on the table.

Sitting up slowly, he took a long look at the man sitting opposite him. Despite the crazy proposal—and seriously, it was *crazy* in every sense of the word—he could see that Seth was genuine in his offer. Giving himself a mental shake, he took a sip of whisky before meeting Seth's eyes.

"You're one hundred percent serious about this, aren't you?"

Seth nodded in reply.

"So, let me get this straight; you want to marry me and then gift me your inheritance of one hundred thousand dollars? And we'll have to be married for a year?"

"Yes. Like you said, I don't need the money. I make that in interest in a good month, so really, it's not going to affect me to give it to you, and then you'll be debt free and have some left over to help while you look for another job."

"And our marriage would be one of convenience only. A business transaction?" Cal was surprised at the stab of disappointment he felt at the thought. "Why marry me at all? Why not just give me a loan? You've admitted you don't need the money, so why go through the hassle of marrying me just to get a hundred thousand dollars?"

Heat gathered in Seth's eyes, and he leaned across the table again, taking Cal's hand in his. Warmth spread through Cal at the gentle swipe of Seth's thumb across the back of his hand.

"It doesn't have to be," Seth said quietly. Cal must have looked confused because Seth continued. "It doesn't have to be a marriage of convenience. We already know we're attracted to each other, and that very brief, too short kiss we shared in Dallas showed we've got chemistry."

"Too sh... short kiss?" Cal stammered as the memory of Seth's lips on his flared bright in his mind.

"Way too damn short," Seth growled, his eyes darkening.

"Again, though. Why marry me? If you just want sex, then we don't need to get married."

"True, but I like the idea of being married to you. There's something about you that has gotten under my skin, and I want to spend time with you and get to know you better."

"Seth, you're not making sense," Cal said tiredly. He hated to beleaguer the point, but he was truly at a loss as to why Seth was offering to help him out. Sure, they had a mutual attraction, but marriage?

Seth squeezed his hand gently. "Cal, please, trust me. Yes, I could just sleep with you, and I could just give you the money to clear your debts, but I have my reasons."

Seth didn't elaborate, and to be honest, Cal was too tired to dig further. "I'd want certain conditions in place if I agree to this hare-brained scheme."

"Of course," Seth agreed quickly. "Whatever you want."

"Careful, Seth, I could ask for anything," Cal teased back.

"I trust you, Cal. You wouldn't take advantage."

"How do you know that?"

"Because if you were someone who would take advantage, you'd have already hit Sarge and Jax up for the money."

At the mention of his cousin and Jax, alarm ricocheted through him.

"Ah, fuck!" He ran a hand down his face. "Sarge and Jax. What will they say? God, what will *everyone* say?"

"Who cares what they say or think? This is between us and is no one else's business."

"But, Seth, you're... *you!*"

"I know I'm me," Seth replied dryly.

"No! I mean, you're *the* Seth Worthington, the hot lead guitarist for Larkspur, one of the biggest bands in the world."

"And you're Callahan Stevens, the sexy tech geek and current assistant to the PA of Larkspur. I'm not seeing the problem here, Cal. We're just two guys who are helping each other out."

Cal slumped into his chair. He wasn't going to win this argument. Could he do it? Could he marry for money? Because basically, that's what it came down to. As Seth had said, it was all very nineteenth century.

"What happens when the year is up? Do we divorce and go our separate ways? Where are we going to live? Do we make this look like a real marriage to the outside world?"

"Cal, babe, calm down," Seth soothed. "It's okay. One thing at a time." Cal nodded and Seth squeezed his hand again. "To answer your questions; I don't know, I don't know, at my house in California, I'd like it to be a real marriage."

Cal's tired brain matched the answers to his questions and stalled when he got to the last one. "You want to make this a proper marriage? As in, sleeping in the same bed and—" he waved a hand in the air.

"Yes, an actual marriage, including sleeping in the same bed, and," Seth flashed him a look that turned his insides to mush, "everything and anything that may happen in that bed."

Cal took a moment to process that. Seth wanted a real marriage? Pros and cons of that flooded Cal's mind, but he couldn't really process them right then. Instead, he went with the main thing that concerned him.

"I'd want an agreement in writing. I want you protected, Seth."

"Why would I need to be protected?" The surprise on Seth's face was evident.

"I want a prenup that states that I'm only getting the hundred thousand dollars and nothing else. When the year is up, and we go our separate ways, that is all I take away from the marriage. I don't want people to say I'm only with you for your money and fame."

Seth stared at him thoughtfully before nodding. "Deal."

"D... deal?"

"Yep. Deal. I'll get my brother on it straight away."

"Your brother?" Cal was back to being confused and dazed. He didn't even know how many siblings Seth had, let alone anything else other than what was in the public domain about Seth Worthington of Larkspur. He knew very little about the man behind the rebel rock star persona.

Seth stood and dropped a few bills onto the table before clasping Cal's hand and hauling him to his feet.

"My brother, Art. He's my lawyer. Come on, I can ring him now, and he'll have the paperwork ready by the time we get there."

Cal stumbled after Seth, his feet and brain trying to catch up with the man. "Get where?"

"His office in LA. We'll fly to him first thing tomorrow, and he can have all the paperwork organized for us to sign and then fly back again."

Cal stopped moving, causing Seth to lose grip of his hand. He took another few steps before realizing he was alone. He turned to face Cal.

"Come on. Why have you stopped?"

"Why have I stopped?" Cal asked incredulously.

"Yes. We need to get moving."

"You want to do all of this now? Right now?"

"Well, there's no point in leaving it any later, and besides, we're in Las Vegas. Where else can you get married on short notice?"

Cal shook his head in resignation. What the hell was he getting into?

CHAPTER TEN

S eth strode towards the concierge desk, Cal scurrying by his side. The poor guy looked poleaxed, but admittedly, Seth had blindsided him with his suggestion to get married.

He knew it was a crazy idea, but it was one that helped them both.

He came to a stop in front of the VIP desk and nodded at the welcoming smile of the man behind it.

"Good evening, Mr. Worthington. How may I be of assistance to you?"

"Good evening. I need a charter helicopter for two passengers to LAX as soon as possible and a car to meet us there, please."

"Certainly, Sir. Will you have any luggage?"

"No. We'll be back tomorrow and anything we require, we can get in Los Angeles."

The concierge tapped away at the computer on his desk before nodding.

"I can have you on a flight at 7am. Does that work for you?"

Seth heard Cal gasp next to him and reached for his hand. Cal's hand was slightly clammy and had a fine tremor running through it.

"Yes, that's fine, thank you."

"May I inquire about the other passenger's name?"

"Cal Stevens," Seth replied. He reluctantly let go of Cal's hand and reached for his wallet. He pulled out a credit card and passed it to the concierge.

"Please put all charges on that," he instructed.

"Thank you, Sir."

Cal tugged at Seth's sleeve, and Seth leaned his head close to Cal's to give them some privacy.

"Seth, how much is this going to cost? Do we have to do this now? Can't we wait until the tour break after the Denver concert?"

"No, we need to do it now and don't worry about the cost. I can pay for it."

"Dammit, Seth. That is not the point!" Cal replied in an angry whisper.

"I know it's not, but don't worry about it, okay?"

Trying not to grin at Cal's cute growl of frustration, Seth returned his attention to the concierge.

"All booked, Mr. Worthington," he said, returning Seth his credit card. "A helicopter will land on the hotel helipad. I will get one of the hotel staff to accompany you to the roof when it is here."

"Perfect. Thank you for your help," Seth replied. "If you could, please call up to my room when it's ready."

With a nod of confirmation, Seth reached for Cal's hand as he turned towards the elevator. Surprisingly, Cal didn't protest, and Seth liked the feeling of Cal's palm in his. He gently tugged him across the crowded lobby and managed to time their arrival at the elevator just as one emptied. Seth hurried them into it and pressed the button for their floor. As the doors closed, he risked a glance at Cal and found the younger man staring blankly at the carpeted floor.

Seth stepped in front of him and gently raised his chin. Dark green eyes met his, full of wariness.

"Hey," Seth said gently. "We've got a few hours before we leave. Have you eaten? We can order some food."

"I ate at the arena," Cal replied, "but don't let that stop you from ordering if you're hungry."

The elevator opened on their floor before Seth could reply. He ushered them out and was a few steps down the corridor when he realized Cal wasn't with him. He pivoted to find Cal hesitating behind him.

"What's wrong?"

"Um... my room is that way," Cal replied, hitching a thumb over his shoulder.

Seth noticed the tiredness that made Cal's shoulders slump. A glance at his phone made him blink at the time. It was after two in the morning. No wonder Cal was looking exhausted. Seth's protective instincts were kicking in. He wanted to tuck Cal up in bed, preferably next to him, and let the man rest. It was on the tip of his tongue to offer for Cal to come back to his room, where he could keep an eye on him, but something in Cal's demeanor made him pause. He didn't want to push too hard and frighten him away.

He laid a hand on Cal's shoulder. "Tell you what, you go grab a few hours of sleep. Come to my room at six thirty. I can order us a light breakfast before we leave at seven."

"What time do you think we'll be back? I need to let Jax know I'm not going to be available in the morning." Cal chewed worriedly on his bottom lip. Seth gently thumbed his chin, making him stop.

"We should be back mid-afternoon. Plenty of time to get married before we hit the road for Denver," he told him softly.

Cal swallowed deeply and then nodded his agreement.

"What am I going to tell Jax? And Sarge. What will Sarge do?"

"Tell them the truth," Seth replied and was surprised at the stab of hurt when Cal looked horrified at the idea. "I know Jax and Sarge are your family, but in a way, they're mine too, and I'd like to think I know them pretty well. They'll be shocked, yes, but they love you and even though I drive them both crazy at times, they know I wouldn't do anything to hurt you."

Cal didn't look convinced, so Seth pushed a little further. "Cal, if the idea of being married to me is so bad, then we don't have to do it."

"No, I agreed, but I just...." Cal paused to yawn widely before blushing as he apologized.

"Look, a hotel hallway is not the best place for this discussion, so go and grab some sleep, and we'll pick it up again in the morning, okay?" Seth gave in to temptation and pressed a gentle kiss between Cal's furrowed brows.

"Yeah, okay," Cal agreed, looking unsure of what to do next.

"Do you want me to walk you to your room?"

"No. I'm good. Thanks." With a small smile, Cal turned and headed away. Seth watched him keenly, anxious to make sure he got to his room safely.

Cal shoved his sunglasses up his nose as the early morning glare of LA's sunlight bounced off the glass-clad high-rises. He felt like he was having an out-of-body experience as Seth led them to the entrance of an imposing tower block.

He murmured his thanks as Seth held the door for him and then walked beside him towards the bank of elevators.

How was he here? Twenty-four hours ago, he'd been preparing for Larkspur's second Vegas show and going about his business, and now he was heading to a lawyer's office to sign a prenuptial agreement before flying back to Vegas to get married.

He leaned heavily against the elevator wall, suppressing a yawn. He'd only managed about two hours of fitful sleep. His conscience had not wanted to let him leave without telling Jax and Sarge what was happening. That brief phone call had resulted in both of them in his room and his cousin falling into complete Marine mode. It had taken some fast talking by Cal to stop the man from going to kill his future husband. He could still hear Jax's voice now.

"What do you mean you're marrying Seth? I didn't realize you'd been dating," Jax said as she stared at where he sat dejectedly on the end of the bed. He really didn't need this. He just wanted to sleep!

"Seth doesn't date, he fucks around," Sarge growled, hands on hips. *"He usually has a groupie in every damn city we play in."*

Jealousy stabbed through Cal at the thought of Seth with someone else. He knew the man was no saint, but Cal felt sick at the thought that not an hour ago, the man had proposed to him. Had he come from a fan's bed and seen Cal and taken pity on him?

"Cal!" Jax's voice pulled him from his thoughts. *"Honey. You don't have to marry Seth just to get the money. We can loan it to you."*

"No! Definitely not," Cal protested. *"You've done more than enough to help me out."*

"But getting married. To Seth, of all people. You think that's your best option to fix this?"

"Yes. I do." He sighed. *"I know it's unconventional, but it helps us both out. I could have lied and told you that we'd fallen madly in love, but it was Seth that told me to tell you the truth. I know his reputation. I'm not stupid, but it's only for a year, and I've insisted on a prenup, so he's protected."*

"So he's *protected? Why would you want to protect him?"* Sarge asked.

"Because I don't want people thinking I'm only with him for his money."

Sarge had raised an eyebrow, which had Cal groaning.

"Yes, I am fully aware of the irony, but you know what I mean."

Sarge had crouched down in front of him. *"Cal. Are you sure about all of this?"*

"Yes," he replied. And he was. He didn't know why he was, but he felt like it was the right thing to do.

"Okay then. Just promise me that if, for whatever reason, you want out, you come to us first. We're your family, and we're always here for you."

"Thanks, Sarge. Seth's a good guy. I wouldn't be doing this if I didn't think that."

"We know he's a good guy. We're just worried."

"Thanks. I know. I love you guys."

After hugs and promises to call them as soon as he got back from LA, they'd left him. His alarm had gone off way too quickly, and after a quick shower, he'd made his way to Seth.

As promised, there had been a light breakfast ready in Seth's room, and Cal had mainlined as much coffee as he could in the short time they had before going to the hotel roof where their private helicopter had been waiting. And now, here they were, in LA.

The elevator door slid open with an unobtrusive whoosh, Seth gently pushing Cal ahead of him into the bright reception area of his brother's law offices. Worthington Frank and Associates were on the twentieth floor and had a good view of the city.

The receptionist greeted them with a smile. "Good morning, Mr. Worthington, Mr. Stevens."

"Good morning, Stella," Seth replied. "I presume Art is waiting for us?"

"Yes, he said to go on back once you got here. He's in his office, and fresh coffee and pastries are available."

"You're too good for him, Stella," Seth told her with a wink.

"Oh, don't worry, he knows," she replied with a grin.

Cal thanked her and followed Seth down a short corridor towards an open office door.

"She seems nice," he commented.

"Yeah. Art has been my lawyer ever since he passed the bar, and he's the personal lawyer for all of us in the band. Stella has been with him since the beginning, following him from his first job when he set up on his own. Her name should be on the company header because she's the one that really runs the place."

"And I am forever grateful that she does," said a deep voice from across the room.

Cal found himself blinking at the tall, dark-haired man who was clearly Seth's brother. They had similar coloring and facial features, but Art's shoulders were a little wider, and his muscles were the product of a gym, whereas Seth was wirier, with a leaner body. Art's bespoke suit generously showcased the man's body in the same way that Seth's soft, faded jeans and beaten leather jacket did. Either way, both men had been hit hard with the good-looking stick.

A happy grin suffused Seth's face, which was mirrored on his brothers as they met in the middle of the spacious office for a tight hug.

"Good to see you, brother," Art said, stepping out of the embrace. He turned towards Seth, extending his hand. "Hi, Cal. Good to meet you."

"Hi. Likewise."

Art waved them towards a comfortable-looking couch and chair arrangement. On the low table between them was a pot of fragrant coffee and a plate of fresh pastries. Seth's hand landed on his lower back, urging him across the room.

Cal dropped onto the couch, making room for Seth to join him, relishing the warm strength of the man next to him. He still wasn't sure what the hell he was doing, but the alternative of a tanked credit rating and excessive loan payments wasn't one he wanted to think about.

"Coffee, Cal?" Art asked, leaning over the table.

"Please," Cal replied with a smile. Art seemed nice, and he obviously adored his brother from the happy smile that he wore.

They settled into their seats with coffee, and heat prickled under Cal's skin as Art quietly appraised him. Cal shifted uncomfortably and stiffened when Seth dropped his arm across Cal's shoulders. He could feel Seth's keen gaze on him, and he suddenly felt trapped with the twin stares of the Worthington brothers pinning him in place.

"Cal, from what little Seth has told me, you seem like a nice guy. You look relatively sane, so forgive me for asking, are you sure you want to marry my brother?"

"Um... thanks, I think?" Cal replied. The twinkle of amusement in Art's eyes had him relaxing a little. "And, yes, I am relatively sane, or at least I was until I started working for Larkspur."

Art grinned at him. "You didn't answer my question."

"Damn lawyers," Seth muttered, but Cal could hear the teasing tone in his voice.

"Well, really, no, I'm not sure I want to marry him," Cal replied and patted Seth's thigh when he tensed next to him, "but he really is the lesser of two evils, and they do say better the devil you know."

"And just how *well* do you know my brother?"

"Art," Seth growled, "he's not on the witness stand. This is a good option for both of us. I get to fulfill Aunt Rosemary's will conditions and Cal gets his loans paid off."

Cal leaned forward and placed his coffee cup on the table before resting his elbows on his knees. "Art, I understand your concerns, and I totally agree with them. I'd be worried too if my brother suddenly announced he was getting married to a virtual stranger and was doing it for money."

"Do you have a brother?" Seth interrupted.

"Yeah, two, both older," Cal replied distractedly.

"Huh," Seth said, and Art rolled his eyes.

"You don't even know the basics about each other. How is this marriage going to work?" Art demanded.

"Art, why are you making a big deal out of this? I need to get married, and if we do, he can get the money he needs. We're not fooling ourselves into thinking that this is the love match of the century. Kellet and Jamie have got that market cornered. Please, just do the paperwork, and we'll get out of your hair."

"It's not quite as simple as that, Seth," Art stated.

"Well, make it simple, big brother. That's what I pay you for."

With a sigh, Art stood and crossed to his desk, returning with a slim folder. He resumed his seat and pulled out a sheaf of papers before reaching into his jacket pocket for a gold pen.

"I just need to clarify a couple of things, and then Stella will run off the final paperwork for you to sign, okay?"

At their nods, Art began to go through the clauses of the agreement.

"Right, to inherit the bequest of Rosemary Stanaway, you, Seth Worthington, must marry within three years of her death and remain married for a period no shorter than twelve months. Once the period of twelve months has passed, the sum of one hundred thousand dollars will be credited to an account of your choosing."

Seth nodded his agreement, but Cal held up a hand before Art could continue.

"Yes, Cal?"

"Seth doesn't get the money until after we've been married a year?"

"That's right. Although this is an antiquated bequest, it is standard that no monies are paid until the terms are met in full."

"Did you know this?" he asked Seth.

"I knew I had to be married for a year before I could get the money, yes."

Cal sat silently as the implications raced through his brain. If Seth didn't get the money right away, it meant that he couldn't give it to Cal, which meant he was still going to be in a fuck ton of debt.

Art must have realized where Cal's thoughts were going. "Don't worry, Cal. Tomorrow, I'll authorize the transfer from

Seth's account to yours, and then, in a year, I'll transfer the money from Aunt Rosemary's estate to Seth."

"I can afford it, Cal. Please stop worrying," Seth reassured him.

Cal gave a shaky nod, and Art returned to the papers in his hand.

"Okay, so we're clear that Seth will transfer one hundred thousand dollars to you, Cal. I have here the agreement that states the details." Art paused and frowned. "Seth also said that you were adamant that the one hundred thousand dollars is all you will take from the marriage when it dissolves."

"Yes, and as soon as I'm able, I'll pay him back. This is just a business transaction."

"I thought we agreed this wasn't a loan?" Seth argued. "I don't want you to pay it back."

Cal stared at him. "I know you don't—"

"Then why are you insisting it's a loan? Please, Cal. Just accept the damn money."

Cal took in the stubborn set of Seth's jaw and reluctantly nodded.

Art looked between them both before continuing. "You're a software developer, I believe?"

"Yes. I was working for Crinkle Media, which was bought out by Systems Corp. I was made redundant and haven't been able to find a job yet in the industry."

Art made a note before returning his gaze to Cal's. "What were the terms of your redundancy?"

"Um, basically they waived the non-compete clause and promised a payout of six months' salary."

"Which they haven't paid," Seth growled, drawing a surprised glance from his brother.

"What do you mean?"

Cal sighed. "They haven't paid a cent of the severance pay, which is why we're here today."

"Do you have a copy of the agreement?"

"Yeah. I can email you a copy," Cal replied. "Why? Will it affect the agreement between Seth and me?"

"No, not at all. I'm concerned that an organization as big as Systems Corp has not upheld their end of the agreement. I presume you've tried contacting them?"

"Numerous times. I've got a couple of form email replies back, saying they're working on it, but the last few times, there's been no response."

Art tapped the end of the pen against his chin before noting something else on the papers in front of him. "Can you send me copies of all the correspondence as well? I'll get one of my team on it."

"Oh, but... " Cal began to protest and stopped when Seth's hand firmly squeezed his arm.

"Shh, Cal. Art's got this." Before Cal could continue to protest, Art grinned at him.

"Don't worry about the cost. I'll put it on Seth's bill."

"No, I can't let you do that," Cal said, looking between the brothers, who had matching grins.

"Sure I can. In a few hours, you'll be family, and what's Seth's is yours."

"No! That's the whole point of this meeting. I don't want anything else of Seth's. Hell, I don't even want his money, but I can't let my credit rating drop, and I'm just so tired of worrying about it all." Cal stopped as the admission slipped out.

Seth's arm slid around his shoulders, and he was pulled into the warmth of the man's side. A soft kiss pressed against his temple.

"Relax, Cal. It's all going to work out."

Art hummed, and Cal saw an unreadable look on his face. It quickly cleared, though, as the lawyer smiled and nodded. "Don't worry, Cal. I'll get these to Stella, and we'll have everything ready to go shortly. Then we can head back to Vegas and get you two married off."

"We?" Seth asked.

"Ha, you don't think I was going to let you get married without being there to witness it, did you, little brother? This is a momentous occasion, and besides, it will make it easier for me to finalize all the details if I'm there."

Cal's mind tuned out as Seth and Art ironed out the final details. He still wasn't sure he was doing the right thing, but he honestly couldn't see another way out of the mess he was in. He couldn't ask family; his parents were comfortable financially, but they weren't able to help him out. They'd helped him with his living costs while he was in college, but all the tuition fees were his responsibility. His brothers weren't in a position to help either, so that avenue was closed.

A soft touch stroking his cheek had his eyes opening, and he sat up with a jolt, realizing he'd dropped off to sleep. Seth was smiling at him warmly, and Cal felt his face heat.

"Sorry, didn't mean to doze off," he apologized.

"It's all good," Art reassured him as he sat down in the seat opposite. "From what Seth says, you didn't get much sleep last night."

Cal reached for the glass of water on the table and took a small sip to cover his embarrassment at falling asleep during an important meeting.

"Okay, all the paperwork is ready to go," Art said, placing several pages on the table.

Cal blinked. How long had he been out?

"Cal, if you can just read through this and let me know if there are any changes you want to make?"

Giving himself a mental shake to wake up, Cal slowly read through the contract. Everything he'd asked for was listed—which wasn't much, but still, it was the principle of the matter. He reread everything again twice before nodding at Art.

"Yeah, this looks all good," he said, reaching for the pen on the table. "I just have to sign here and here and then initial each page?"

Art grinned at him, and Cal wasn't sure why. "What? Did I miss something?" he asked before skimming over the contract again. He didn't think he had, but hey, he was operating on very little sleep.

"No, you're one of the first people I've ever met that read every line of the agreement, not once, but three times," Art replied.

"My brother finds thoroughness sexy," Seth said, throwing a look at Art that suspiciously looked like a warning.

Art raised his hands in defense. "Hey, it is, right up there with consent."

"And we're both consenting adults, who've consented to a marriage of convenience, so back off, big brother," Seth growled.

"Mmm, hmm," Art replied, amusement dancing in his eyes.

Cal looked between the two men. Something was going on, but he couldn't be bothered to try to work out what it was. He returned his attention to the paperwork in front of him and began signing and initialing where he had to.

A few minutes later, Seth signed the last page of the contract with a flourish and sat back with a satisfied grin on his face.

"There you go, Art. All signed and sealed."

"Thanks. I'll get Stella to file everything, and then we can look into flying back to Las Vegas. In the meantime, Seth, jump on my computer and apply for your marriage license. Then we only have to turn up at the courthouse with your ID, and we'll be good to go."

Seth watched his brother leave the office before turning towards Cal.

"You okay?"

"Yeah, just tired," Cal reassured him with a soft smile. "I... I know I keep saying this but thank you. You really didn't have to do all this, and well, it means a lot."

"You don't have to keep thanking me. You're helping me out too, remember? Let's just get today over with and then we can work out all the other stuff."

Seth pushed to his feet and held out a hand. "Come on, let's jump online and get all the paperwork sorted."

Cal let himself be pulled from the couch and led over to Art's desk. Seth pulled out the leather executive chair and gently pushed Cal down into it.

"What are you doing?"

"You're the computer guy, not me. Do your thing," Seth told him, waving a hand at the desktop computer.

"Really?" Cal asked with a raised eyebrow. "Are you telling me you don't know how to get online?"

"No, I'm not saying that at all. Just, this is your area of expertise, and you'll be a lot quicker at the typing thing. I am, at best, a two-finger typist who uses the hunt-and-peck method."

Cal gave a mock shudder, his eyes twinkling with amusement. "Yeah, that would make me break out in hives. Having to watch that would be torture."

Seth grinned, glad his little distraction plan was working, as Cal woke up the screen. His grin grew as he heard a muttered curse under Cal's breath.

"What was that?"

"We need his password to log in."

"Oh, that's easy," Seth said, leaning over the keyboard. "It's ArtSet27" he said as he typed, and the screen cleared.

"You have your brother's password?" Cal said, a disgusted tone in his voice. "And he's a lawyer? I expected better from him."

"We have each other's passwords, y'know, for if anything happens to the other, we can access and clear each other's browser history."

Cal just muttered something indecipherable as his fingers flew across the keyboard, and within seconds he was on the correct website, and the form they needed was on the screen. Seth pushed down the tendril of desire that snaked through him. Who knew someone typing could be sexy? Or rather, Cal typing was sexy, as was the way his tongue poked out of the corner of his very kissable mouth.

And now Seth was thinking about kissing his future husband. *Huh, husband.* He'd never really thought about having a life partner, despite the terms of Rosemary's will, but now, the thought of the sexy blond in front of him had him wanting things he'd never thought he'd wanted. He watched as Cal's slim fingers danced across the keys, as quickly and familiarly as his own did on a fretboard. A sudden vision of his ring on Cal's finger popped up, and he found he wanted that, too. Wanted the world to know Cal was off the market, that he was taken.

Cal's voice interrupted his musings, and he gave him the information he needed to complete the form. It didn't take long, and Cal submitted everything he needed to before closing out of the site.

"Is there anything else we need to do?" Seth asked just as Art returned.

"Have you chosen a chapel to get married in?" his brother asked with a grin. "Are you going to keep to a music theme and get an Elvis impersonator to marry you?"

Before either Cal or Seth could reply, their phones chimed with incoming messages. Seth dug his out of his pocket and saw it was a message from Miles. He frowned. It was unusual for their manager to message them directly; usually, Jax did it.

He swiped the screen open and read the brief message as a gasp came from Cal. He reread the message before looking up at Cal.

"Well, that's going to make things fun," he said.

Cal pushed away from the desk and stood. "I... I should be there. Jax will need my help."

"What's happened?" Art asked. "Is there anything I can do?"

"Pictures of Jamie and Kellet acting a little more than friendly have been posted online," Seth told him. "Miles says it's being handled by the label's lawyers, but to be aware and not to comment."

Seth quickly found the pictures online and was relieved to see they were nothing more than the couple holding hands and another of them kissing in an elevator.

"What are we going to do?" Cal asked, a worried look on his face.

"There's nothing we can do. Miles and Jax have it under control. I say we carry on as we planned. This will all blow over in the next couple of days and life will return to normal."

Cal didn't look convinced, and Seth looked to his brother for help, only to find him regarding them with a familiar look on his face.

"What are you thinking, Art? I know that look."

"Well, there are a couple of options. If you go public with your marriage, it will take the heat off Jamie and Kellet, but it won't be pretty."

"Or....?"

Art hitched a hip onto the corner of his desk, crossing his arms. "Or, you keep this completely under the radar for now. Let things settle with the guys, and then, maybe after the tour is over, announce your marriage."

Seth looked at Cal in askance. Cal chewed his lip as he thought. It was obviously a nervous habit he had, and like last night, Seth gently tugged at his chin, making him release it.

"What are you thinking, Cal? I'm happy to go with whichever you're most comfortable with." Seth was happy with either option Art had suggested but wanted Cal to make the decision.

"I vote for the second option," Cal said after a few more moments of thinking. "Is that okay?" he asked Seth.

"Yes. Whatever you want. Jax and Miles are going to have enough to do without us adding fuel to the fire."

Cal looked stricken at that thought, but Seth reassured him. "They've dealt with worse. Stop worrying. We'll announce our marriage at the end of the tour. By then, things will have settled with Jamie and Kel, and we'll be able to hide at home and not get bugged by the press like we would if we were on tour."

Cal reluctantly nodded his agreement, and Seth smiled at his brother. "Come on, we've got a wedding to get to."

CHAPTER ELEVEN

"A nd do you, Callahan Andrew Stevens, take Seth Joseph Worthington, to be your lawfully wedded husband?"

The marriage celebrant's voice was low and melodic, instilling a sense of calm in Cal. Seth's hands were warm and strong as they gently gripped his own as they stood in Seth's hotel suite. Art was their only witness, and the officiant had signed a non-disclosure agreement without any concern.

With more confidence than he was feeling, he nodded. "I do."

With a smile, the celebrant turned to Seth and repeated the question. Seth gave a wicked grin as he replied, and Cal felt Seth was enjoying this a little too much for someone entering a marriage of convenience.

"Do you have the rings?"

Rings? Cal's panicked gaze swung first to Seth and then to Art, who stepped forward and passed a ring to Seth.

Seth gave Cal's hand a squeeze before a cool band of metal slid onto the ring finger of his left hand. He vaguely heard Seth repeating the words the celebrant was saying, but his focus was on the plain, wide gold band that somehow fit perfectly. *Oh, God. This is real. I'm getting married*.

"Cal?"

Seth's voice pulled him from his panicked thoughts. Art was looking at him sympathetically and holding another plain gold band for him. Cal gave what he hoped was a reassuring smile and took the ring. He pushed the ring onto Seth's finger, sliding it easily over the knuckle to rest snugly at the base. It looked slightly out of place next to the other chunky rings Seth always wore.

With a shaky breath, he repeated the traditional vows about honor and love. They'd decided to stick with the basics, as it was quicker and easier and less likely to cause suspicion with the officiant, although Cal was sure they'd overseen many other weddings that were based on a lot less than his and Seth's.

Seth had asked him if he wanted Jax and Sarge there, but Cal had declined. They were busy doing damage control on the Jamie and Kellet situation. Besides, this wasn't a real wedding. Well, of course, it was *legal*, but in terms of marrying someone he loved, then, no, it wasn't what he'd imagined.

"By the power vested in me by the state of Nevada, I now declare you married," the officiant said with a smile. "You may kiss your husband."

Cal had a brief second to register that Seth was leaning towards him before warm lips pressed against his own. His hands clutched at Seth's shirt as Seth held him steady with strong hands on his upper arms. The kiss only lasted a few seconds, but it was enough to send tendrils of heat through his body.

"Congratulations Mr. and Mr. Worthington," Art said with a grin, clapping Seth on the back. "Or, is it Mr. and Mr. Stevens? Or are you going to hyphenate? Worthington-Stevens? Stevens-Worthington?" he mused.

"Um...," Cal looked wildly at Seth. "We haven't discussed names."

"It's something we can discuss when we're home in LA," Seth reassured him.

"Champagne, anybody?" Art asked as he returned to the room after seeing the officiant out.

Cal shook his head. "Just soda water for me, please." He nodded towards the bathroom. "Excuse me for a minute?"

"Take all the time you need," Seth replied with a gentle smile.

Closing the bathroom door behind him, Cal leaned against the sink and stared at his reflection. He was so tired. He'd had about six hours of sleep in the last twenty-four hours, and most of that had been made up of naps while traveling. Even by his standards, he was pale, and the bags under his eyes could give the band's equipment trunks a run for their money. Certainly not a look any groom expected to have on their wedding day.

After using the facilities, he took a moment to gather himself. They were due to be on the tour bus in a few hours, and he really needed to check in with Jax and make sure everything was running smoothly, but God, all he wanted to do was sleep. He splashed some water on his face to try and perk himself up. He could sleep on the bus. The beds may be compact cubby holes, but right now, he could sleep standing up. After a last look in the mirror, he returned to the main room. At his entry, Seth and Art broke off from what looked like a heated discussion.

"Is everything okay?" Cal asked cautiously. "Has something else happened with the band?"

"No, Cal. Everything is fine," Seth reassured him.

"Oh, that's... that's good then." Cal was unconvinced, but he let it ride. "I suppose we ought to be getting ready to go. I need to check in with Jax before we leave."

"Cal, you're dead on your feet. I'm sure Jax can cope for a night," Art said, ignoring the glare his brother was sending his way.

"What's going on?" Cal asked, looking between the brothers.

"Art thinks you should go back to LA with him," Seth explained.

"And Seth doesn't agree," Art retorted.

Cal sank into the couch, his gaze switching from brother to brother as they argued back and forth.

"Why?"

His quiet question managed to silence them. There was a long pause before Seth sighed and waved a hand at Art to explain.

"You have a twelve-hour bus ride to Denver, and you're already running on very little sleep. No offense, but you'll be at less than your best, and it's the last show before the mid-tour break. Come back to LA with me, catch up on some rest and then we can tackle your problem with Systems Corp right away."

Cal was unsure how to respond. He looked to Seth, who sighed and dropped onto the couch next to him, taking his hand and gently twisting the shiny new band on Cal's ring finger.

"I know this is a marriage of convenience, but I wanted to spend our first night as husbands together."

Cal stared at him. *Did he mean….?*

"Wait, that sounds wrong. What I mean is that we've not had much time alone together, and I want to get to know you better."

Cal was surprised to see a hint of red creep up Seth's face as he admitted this.

"But you won't be able to do that on the bus if you're not letting anyone know about your marriage," Art interjected, making his brother glare at him again. He turned to Cal. "What would *you* like to do?"

"Sleep," Cal said, the word slipping out before he had a chance to filter it.

"That settles it then," Art said with a satisfied grin. "You come back with me, and Seth can carry on with the band. He'll fly back to LA from Denver and then you can begin your married life together."

Seth gave Cal a searching glance before reluctantly nodding in agreement. "Okay then, but I'll fly back with you tonight and get you settled in my place."

"But you're supposed to be on the bus to Denver in, like, two hours," Cal protested.

"I'll catch a flight tomorrow and meet the band there."

"But, the cost...."

"Cal, one thing you'll discover about my brother is that despite all outward appearances, he's actually a bit of a scrooge, and he rarely spends any money at all. Unless," he added slyly, "it's something or someone he cares about."

Seth gave his brother a baleful glare, which Art ignored. "I'll ring Stella now and get her to make all the arrangements. You two let whoever you've got to know and get your bags sorted."

Cal slumped into the couch as the brothers grabbed their phones to make their respective calls. His bags were already packed and ready to go, and Seth was talking with Miles. He fired a text off to Jax, knowing she'd be too busy to take his call, to let her know his change of plans and promising to call once he'd arrived in LA.

CHAPTER TWELVE

S eth pushed open the large door into the foyer of his home in Cold Water Canyon. He stood back to let Cal pass him and watched as he took in the wide open space. Cal's mouth gaped slightly as he took in the double staircase that curved on each side of the foyer.

"Wow." The quiet exclamation had him smiling at Cal.

"Yeah, I know," he said, a rare wave of embarrassment washing through him. The house was huge and way too much for one person, but it had been one of his first purchases when Larkspur had made it big, and he'd hoped his parents would see it as a mark of his success and finally realize that he wasn't wasting his time with his music. Of course, they hadn't, and he'd thought about selling a number of times, but he was rarely home and had never got around to it.

"It's... it's...." Cal seemed speechless as he took in the soaring ceilings and marble flooring.

"A lot, I know," Seth admitted, ushering Cal further in. He waved a hand. "This is, like, the formal side of the house. Reception rooms and large dining room." He paused and pointed to a short hallway leading to the left of the stairs. "Kitchen and den are back there, and the games room and the studio are on the opposite side."

"Do you live here alone?"

"More or less. My Aunt Sunny lives in the guest house out the back. She looks after the place when I'm on tour. I have a housekeeper that comes in once a week, but yeah, otherwise, it's just me."

Cal swayed, and Seth reached out a steadying hand. "Come on, I can give you the tour in the morning. Let's get you settled, and you can get some rest."

Seth gently guided Cal up the staircase and along the hallway to his bedroom. He pushed open the door and then hesitated. He knew he'd said he'd wanted to spend time getting to know each other, but Cal looked like death warmed over.

"Um...," he stammered, suddenly feeling uncharacteristically shy. "This is my... ah... room, but if you want to stay in one of the guest rooms, you can."

Cal gave him a small smile. "No, this is fine." Seth searched Cal's face to see if he was comfortable with the arrangements or just being polite. Then again, the poor guy would probably agree to sleeping on the couch if he meant he got to lie down for a while.

Seth tugged his hand and led him further into the room. "Bathroom is just through there. There are plenty of towels and stuff, so just help yourself."

"Thanks. I think I'd fall asleep in the shower, so I won't risk it. I'll just brush my teeth."

"Sure. I'll leave you to it then."

"Wait! Where are you going?" Cal's surprised question stopped him on his way to the door.

"I'm just going to lock up and grab us some water. I'll be back in a few minutes."

"Oh. Okay then. Good." Cal nodded before opening his bag and taking out a shaving bag and a change of clothes.

Seth made his way back downstairs and after checking the front door was secure and the alarm set, he headed towards the kitchen. The room was dimly lit by the under-cabinet lighting, casting warm shadows across the room. A small posy of flowers sat in a mason jar in the center of the diner-style booth that made up the dining nook. He grinned at the sight. Aunt Sunny's doing. He'd messaged his aunt earlier, in between flights, to let her know he'd be home for a few hours and that he had a guest staying.

He knew Art would fill her in on the details in the morning, hopefully before Cal woke up. As he opened the fridge door to grab them some water, the light caught his new ring. The plain, soft-brushed gold band looked out of place next to the chunky silver rings he wore on his middle and forefinger. *Married. He was married.* He wasn't sure what to feel. Part of him was worried he'd coerced Cal into something he didn't want, and the other half was nervously excited about getting to know Cal better.

The thought had him jogging back up the stairs. He quietly pushed the bedroom door open and wasn't surprised to see Cal fast asleep already. He was a little disappointed, but he pushed it away, knowing he'd get to spend time with Cal in a few days after he played the Denver show.

After a quick shower and remembering to set his alarm, he slid into the large California King bed next to his sleeping husband. Propping himself on his elbow, he gazed at the man beside him. Cal murmured and snuffled adorably in his sleep before pulling the duvet up nearly over his head, burying himself beneath the sheets. Seth quietly chuckled before settling down himself, letting Cal's soft snores lull him to sleep.

Morning came too soon, Seth's phone buzzing on the bedside cabinet, dragging him from sleep. He quickly shut it off and glanced over to make sure it hadn't woken Cal. He needn't have worried. There was a burrito-shaped lump next to him. He could just make out the top of Cal's head, his blond hair bright against the navy blue of the pillow. He wanted nothing more than to burrow in beside Cal and gently tease him from sleep.

Was he a morning person? Or did he need a large dose of caffeine, like Seth did, to get going in the morning? Seth pondered the questions as he quietly dressed. Whenever he'd see Cal on tour, he was already hard at work, organizing them onto the bus or into waiting vehicles to take them to the venue, which meant he probably was a morning person.

He scribbled a quick note and left it propped against the bottle of water on the nightstand where Cal would see it when he woke. He was tempted to lean down and press a kiss to the top of Cal's head but didn't want to wake him. With a lingering glance, he left to meet the car waiting to take him back to the airport.

***

Cal woke slowly, his mouth dry and eyes gritty. Pushing the heavy cover off, he yawned and stretched. His body ached, and his head felt wooly. *God, what had he been drinking last night?* Rubbing a hand over his face, he pushed himself up onto his elbow and reached for his phone on the nightstand. Next to it was a bottle of water with a note propped against it. He rubbed at his eye with the heel of his hand, trying to focus as he picked up the note. He frowned at the elegant handwriting.

Cal, Sorry I'm not here to show you around, but like I said last night, make yourself at home. I'll call you when I get to Denver. Rest up, and I'll see you in a few days. Seth.

Memory hit him like a sledgehammer, and with a groan, he dropped onto the pillow.

"It wasn't a dream," he whispered to himself. Raising his left hand, the sight of the gold band adorning his ring finger had him whimpering. "Oh shit. I married Seth yesterday." His stomach churned, and he took some deep breaths to stave off the sudden wave of nausea. He took a deep breath and mentally chided himself. He'd agreed to the marriage. True, he hadn't thought Seth had meant get married right there and then, but it had made sense to do it while in Vegas. It was all going to work out.

When he was sure he wasn't going to throw up, he eased himself into a sitting position and reached for the bottle of water and his cell phone. He took small sips of the tepid water as he contemplated the dark screen of his phone. He knew the second he switched it on, it would blow up with messages and missed calls from Jax and Sarge.

He screwed the lid back onto the bottle and thumbed his phone on. There was no point in avoiding it. As predicted, there were several missed calls and messages from his cousin, his boss, and even worse, their big boss, Miles.

Cal wasn't sure which one was the lesser evil, so he started with Miles. If he was going to be sacked for marrying Seth, then he'd rather hear it from Larkspur's manager than Jax.

He played back the voicemail on speaker, Miles's deep voice echoing in the room.

"Cal, I've just heard from Seth that you and he got married last night. I'm sure I'll hear the entire story soon enough, but Seth has asked that it be kept private for now. He said you'd both share the news after the tour." There was a sigh, and Miles continued, his voice weary. "We're dealing with Kellet and Jamie's situation. Jax will be in touch about anything she needs you for, but otherwise, we don't need you until we pick back up again in Seattle. Enjoy your time off."

Cal frowned as he exited the call. Miles usually exuded confidence and had a *don't-fuck-with-me* vibe, but he sounded off. Cal hoped the Kellet and Jamie situation wasn't turning out to be worse than they'd anticipated when the public discovered that Larkspur's drummer and lead singer were in a relationship.

He checked his messages from Jax and Sarge, and as expected, there was a lot of disappointment that he hadn't been on the bus from Las Vegas last night. He sent them a quick message telling them he was okay and that he'd talk to them later once they reached Denver.

His stomach rumbled, reminding him he'd barely eaten in the last twenty-four hours. Shower, then food, he decided. He hoped Seth had something edible in the house. He wasn't supposed to be back for another four days, so he doubted his housekeeper would have stocked the fridge yet.

Fifteen minutes later, he trod carefully down the stairs. He wasn't really sure where he was going; he hadn't exactly been awake enough to take in everything Seth had said last night. Cal came to a stop in the large, open foyer. The marble floor shone as tendrils of sunlight poked through the tall windows above the front door. There were a couple of occasional tables on each side of the door, and several charcoal sketches graced the walls.

Cal edged away from the stairs and instinct had him turning right and following a hallway towards the back of the house. He noticed that there were several more sketches similar in style. He surmised they must be by the same artist. They were mainly still-life subjects and a couple of landscapes, showing the same scene but one at night and the other during the day.

The end of the hallway opened into a large, bright room with a wall of windows looking out over the canyon. He paused in the doorway, senses overloaded at the explosion of color and warmth the room exuded compared to the quiet austerity of the foyer. There were large comfy couches and two recliners. A large screen television graced one wall, and a bookshelf littered with books, paper, and knickknacks stood against the other. To his right was a large wooden table and behind that was a huge open-plan kitchen that many a chef would give their firstborn for.

Cal drifted toward the kitchen, taking in the stainless-steel appliances and dark granite countertops. The floor was smooth tile, but large rugs softened the look. In one corner, there was a bay window with an old-style diner booth with red leather seats and a Formica top, which looked both out-of-place and yet exactly right at the same time. A jaunty bunch of daisies sat in a jar in the center of the table, adding a whimsical touch.

Cal spotted a gleaming coffee machine and gave a small sigh. He really needed a caffeine kick to get his brain working, and as he shuffled over to it, his sock-clad feet silent on the tile, he prayed it was easy to use.

Five minutes later, he was no closer to coffee, and he felt like crying. Despite several hours of sleep, he was still tired, and was it too much to ask for a damn coffee to kick-start his brain? Turning his back on the unhelpful machine, he moved over to the fridge. As expected, there wasn't a lot of fresh food, but there were some bottles of water. Grabbing one, he unscrewed the lid and had just taken a gulp when someone spoke behind him.

"Oh, good morning. I wasn't expecting you to be awake yet. Art said you'd had a late night and weren't to be disturbed."

Cal jumped at the voice, reflexively squeezing the plastic bottle in his hand. Water squirted from the top, splashing his front and onto the floor.

"Shit!"

"Oh, my goodness. I'm sorry. I didn't mean to startle you," the woman said, putting the bags she was holding onto the dinette table. "I thought I'd be back before you woke. I knew Seth had no food in the house, so I went to get some eggs and things."

"Um, hi," Cal said warily.

"Hi," she replied, giving him a bright smile. "I'm Seth's Aunt Sunny. I live out in the guest house, and Seth messaged me to let me know you were staying last night."

As soon as she said she was Seth's aunt, Cal could see the resemblance. She was tall, with dark blond hair that fell in a long braid down her back. She was dressed in a pretty floral dress with a bright red cardigan draped across her shoulders.

Cal returned the smile. Did she know that her nephew had gotten married?

Before he could introduce himself, a loud yapping and the sound of claws on the tile had Cal looking towards the doorway. He caught a glimpse of dark and tan fur before two small bodies wrapped around his feet, tails wagging excitedly and jumping up towards his knees.

Not wanting to stand on the two miniature dachshunds, he took a step to balance himself, only for his foot to meet the small puddle of water he spilled. Having no traction with his socks on, his foot slid out from under him. With a yelp, he felt himself falling. He twisted, trying to avoid landing on the small dogs, who, thinking it was all a game, yapped louder and wriggled excitedly.

He landed with a thud, cracking his elbow against the tile floor. He managed to keep his head from falling backwards and felt his back and neck wrench. His left foot flung out and caught the bottom edge of the cabinet, sending a bolt of pain up his ankle.

"Lulu! Trixie!" Sunny shouted as she rushed over to where Cal was lying on the floor. She tried shooing the dogs away, but they were now on Cal's chest, snuffling and licking at his face. He raised an arm to shove them away. Sunny scooped them up and quickly put them outside before returning to his side. Their faces pressed against the glass as they whimpered.

"Oh, I'm so sorry," Sunny said, easing him into a seated position. "Are you hurt? Did you hit your head?"

Cal groaned as he rubbed a hand around the back of his neck. "No."

"You're very pale. Where does it hurt?"

"I... I'm okay," he reassured her.

"No, you're not," Sunny retorted. "Sit there a second and catch your breath."

He did as she asked, leaning his head against the fridge, taking a couple of shuddering breaths. Sunny bustled around, wiping up the spilled water with a paper towel, before crouching down next to him.

"Okay, now, tell me where it hurts?"

"I banged my elbow, and my foot hit something. I'm okay though."

"Sunny?" a voice called out.

"In the kitchen, Art," she called back.

Cal looked up as Seth's brother strode into the room, looking all kinds of fine in a gray suit. His cheerful smile slipped, and concern clouded his features as he took in the scene.

"What happened? Cal, are you okay? Why are you on the floor?"

"I spilled some water and then slipped. I'm okay," Cal said, putting both hands on the floor to push himself upright.

"It's all my fault," Sunny told Art, keeping a restraining hand on Cal's shoulder. "I startled him, making him spill his water, and then the demon dogs attacked. He was trying to get out of the way and slipped."

Art crossed to them and slid a hand under Seth's elbow, helping him to stand. Cal couldn't stop the hiss of pain as the muscles in his back spasmed. He staggered and then another bolt of pain shot through his foot, and he would have hit the floor again if Art hadn't caught him.

"Woah! Easy there," Art soothed as he steadied him. Sharp blue eyes that were so like his brother's regarded him keenly. "I think we need a trip to the ER."

"What? No! I'm fine, honestly. I just need some Tylenol and coffee, not necessarily in that order, and to rest for a moment or two."

"No. Nothing to eat or drink until you've been seen by a doctor. Seth's going to be pissed that you're hurt and even more so if you don't get checked out."

Cal opened his mouth to protest again, but a quelling look from Art had him slumping in defeat. He wanted to rewind the clock and return to when life was easy. But realistically, when was that? When he worked sixty-plus hours a week for a company that treated him like trash? Or when he didn't have a mountain of debt and no way to pay it?

"Can you walk?" Art asked softly, his grip gentle but firm on Cal's elbow.

Cal nodded and then shook his head when he tried to put weight on his left foot.

"Lean on me. My car's right out front." Art moved to his left and took his weight as Cal shuffle-hopped towards the foyer.

"Oh, Cal. I'm so, so sorry," Sunny said. "I normally keep the dogs on their leashes if I know there are people around as they're so excitable. I honestly didn't think you'd be up yet."

Her tone was full of remorse, and Cal took pity on her. "It's okay. It's been a busy few days, and I'm not running on all cylinders. It was an accident. I'm sure the doctor will find I'm just bruised and battered and tell me to rest up. I'll be as good as new in a day or so. I promise."

"Aunt Sunny, can you run upstairs and grab Cal's shoes?" Art asked.

With a nod, she took off up the stairs. Art turned to Cal. "Thank you for being so nice to Sunny."

"Why wouldn't I be?" Cal asked, confused.

"She's had a bit of a rough deal in life. She hides it well, but she'll be feeling awful that you're hurt and that she let it happen while Seth isn't here."

"Seth won't be mad at her, will he?" Cal asked. Admittedly didn't know Seth well, but from what he'd seen, Seth wouldn't—or shouldn't—be angry at his aunt for something that was a genuine accident.

"No, he won't be. Once we get to the hospital, I'll call him and explain what's happened."

"Do you have to?" Cal asked. "I really don't want to bother him. There's nothing he can do, and he's busy. He doesn't need to be worrying over nothing."

Art gripped him firmly by the shoulders and shook him gently. "You are not nothing. My brother cares for you. If I don't let him know, he'll be furious."

Cal gave a snort of disbelief. Seth may like him, but care for him? He highly doubted that.

"Whatever you're thinking, stop it. Seth wouldn't marry just anyone, not even to satisfy the terms of Aunt Rose's will."

Cal eyed him skeptically, but Art's gaze brooked no argument, so he nodded his agreement. Sunny returned with his shoes, and with more assurances that he was okay, Cal let himself be ushered into the quiet luxury of Art's Mercedes.

CHAPTER THIRTEEN

S eth stared at his cell phone and the unanswered text messages he'd sent to Cal. He hadn't wanted to call and wake the guy up, but he thought his husband would be awake by now. Maybe he was having second thoughts? Seth didn't like to think so, but it was out of character for Cal not to respond to messages and calls. Even his brother and aunt hadn't responded to him, and worry was tickling at his brain.

He was just about to ring his brother again to find out what was going on when Art's name and picture flashed up on the screen.

"Thank fuck," he said by way of greeting. "I was thinking everyone was ignoring me, or has there been some sort of natural disaster that's stopping my calls and messages from getting through to anyone in California?"

"Hey, Seth. Sorry, they frown on the use of phones in the Emergency Room, and this is the first chance I've had to get away and call."

"Emergency room? What the fuck's happened?" Icy dread washed through him. "Is it Aunt Sunny? Is she okay?"

"No, Sunny is fine." Art blew out a breath. "Um... it's Cal."

Relief rushed through Seth that it wasn't his aunt, but it was quickly dispelled as his brain registered what Art had said.

"Cal?"

"Yeah. He's fine, but there was an accident this morning, and we've been at the hospital for hours."

"Accident?" Seth sunk down onto the hotel room bed as his legs gave out from under him. "Is he... what happened?"

"He slipped on some spilled water—"

Art didn't get any further before Seth interrupted him again.

"He slipped. Are you sure? He's not just saying that, is he? He didn't pass out or anything because he's so tired?"

"From what I can gather, he was getting a drink. Aunt Sunny startled him, and he spilled some water. Then the hellhounds attacked. He slipped, trying to avoid them. He's bruised a tendon in his foot from where it connected with the kitchen cabinet."

"Those damn dogs! He didn't hit his head or anything?"

"No. He's wrenched his back and neck and got a lovely bruise on his elbow, but otherwise, he's fine." Art huffed a laugh. "Well, he's fine if you take out the fact he's as grumpy as you are when he doesn't have coffee, and I think he may be a touch hangry as well."

Seth collapsed backwards onto the bed and ran a hand over his face. "I'll call Miles and tell him what's happened, and then I'll charter a flight back."

"Ah. No."

"Ah. Yes." Seth countered. "My husband is hurt. I need to be home."

"I... um... have a message from your... um husband," Art told him, amusement in his tone.

"You do?"

"Yes, and I quote. '*Tell Seth that if he even thinks about coming home before he's done the Denver show, I will file divorce papers quicker than he can run the riff for* Hard Up For Love.' Unquote." Art chuckled. "Your husband is feisty. I like him."

Seth was equally impressed and annoyed. Cal *was* feisty. It was partly what drew Seth to him. But dammit, he wanted to be there for him.

"I'll get him to call as soon as we get back to your place, I promise," Art said, his voice gentle. His brother knew what Seth would be thinking. "Sunny and I will look after him until you're home."

"Thanks, Art. Don't know what I'd do without you."

"You're welcome. Get some rest and kick ass on stage tomorrow. We'll see you in a few days."

They said their goodbyes and Seth dropped his phone onto his chest. He really wanted to run back to California, but he knew his brother and aunt would take care of him, and Cal was right. He couldn't let down the thousands of people who had paid good money to see Larkspur play.

His phone beeped with a message, and he eagerly snatched it up, only to be disappointed when he saw it was from Wil, who had picked up some of Cal's duties in his absence, reminding him they were leaving for sound-check at nine the next morning. He sent back a thumbs-up emoji before throwing his phone onto the nightstand.

He was tipping the room service waiter when his phone rang. With a hasty thanks, he closed the door to his suite and raced to pick up his phone before the call cut out.

"Cal?"

"Hi, Seth. I... I haven't caught you at a bad time, have I?"

"No. My dinner has just arrived, and I was tipping the waiter." He slumped onto the bed. "How are you? How badly are you hurt?"

"I'm okay." Cal sounded even more tired than he had the previous day, and Seth wished he wasn't a thousand miles away.

"What did the doctors say?"

"Rest, and they've given me painkillers and anti-inflammatories. It's just going to be a matter of time."

Relief washed through Seth that it wasn't more serious. "You take all the time you need. I'll be home in a few days."

"Don't rush back on my account. I'm fine, and your aunt has moved into the guest room, so she's on hand if I need her help."

Seth ignored the first part of Cal's statement. "Make sure you ask her for help, okay?"

"Yeah." Cal's reply was subdued, and it pained Seth not to be there.

"Promise me, Cal. Ask Aunt Sunny for help if you need it."

There was a pause before Cal agreed.

They chatted for a few more minutes before Seth wished him good night and ended the call. He picked at his dinner, his appetite having waned. Just a few more days, and then he'd be home.

Two days later, Seth was leaping out of the car that had ferried him home from the airport, barely thanking the driver. He raced through the front door, dumping his duffle bag and art case at the base of the stairs before striding towards the den.

His aunt gave him a warm smile and pressed a finger to her lips as she nodded towards the couch. Seth's eyes landed on Cal's slumbering form. Seth greedily drank in the sight of flushed cheeks and tousled hair. His left foot resting on a small pile of cushions, wrapped in an elasticized compression bandage. He let out a snuffly snort and relief washed through Seth.

He crossed the room to give his aunt a hug. "Thank you for looking after him," he said, keeping his voice low so as not to wake Cal.

"I'm so sorry, Seth. It was all my fault. I didn't think he'd be up, and I let the dogs off their leash. You know what they're like when they meet someone new."

Seth hushed her. He'd heard the full story from Cal and placed no blame on his aunt or her dogs. "It was an accident. Please stop beating yourself up about it."

"Seth? That you?" Cal's husky voice had Seth rushing to his side. He perched on the edge of the coffee table and brushed a finger along Cal's cheek.

"Hey. How are you feeling?"

"Ugh. I'm okay," Cal replied, his cheeks turning a deeper red as he pushed himself upright. Seth noticed the wince of pain that he tried to hide.

"When did you last take some pain relief?" he asked.

"He's about due for the next lot," Sunny told him. "I'll get you some fresh water, Cal. Seth, do you want anything?"

"Coffee would be good, please."

"Same, please, Aunt Sunny," Cal called after her.

A thrill of happiness went through Seth at Cal's words. "Aunt Sunny, huh?"

"You don't mind, do you?" Cal shuffled on the couch. "She insisted, and well, it just felt right."

"No. It's cool." Seth gestured to Cal's foot. "How's the foot?"

"Sore, but okay. The doc said it should be better in about three weeks."

"And what about your neck and back? Any pain there?"

"It's getting better. Just twinges when I wake up or move too quickly."

"I've told him he needs to have a soak in your spa bath, and then I'll arrange for my massage therapist to come and see him," Sunny said as she returned with a tray laden with coffee, a bottle of water, and some sandwiches.

Seth jumped up to help, taking the tray and placing it on the coffee table. He passed Cal a steaming mug of coffee and smiled when Cal took a deep, appreciative breath before sipping.

"Perfect. Thanks, Aunt Sunny," he told her with a smile.

"You need to eat," she reminded him, nodding towards the plate of sandwiches. "There's enough there for both of you."

Seth shot her a grateful smile as he picked up a sandwich and his coffee. He'd left Denver as early as he could, too anxious to eat. He'd wanted to see Cal as soon as possible and reassure himself that he was okay.

"If you two have everything you need, I'll head home," Sunny told them, gathering her things.

"Thank you for helping me out," Cal said, shifting his position as if he was about to stand up. Seth reached over and placed a firm hand on his shoulder.

"And where do you think you're going?" he asked.

Cal tensed beneath his touch before sighing and relaxing back into the cushions. "I was just—"

"You were just going to sit there and rest," Seth interrupted him. Cal threw him a baleful glare before sipping his coffee again, eyes dropping away from Seth's.

"Thanks, Aunt Sunny." Seth gave his aunt a hug.

"It was the least I could do," she replied. "If it hadn't been for my damn dogs, then poor Cal wouldn't be hurt."

"Sunny, I've told you, it's not your fault," Cal protested.

"He's right," Seth agreed. "It was an accident."

"Yes, but..." she broke off when Seth raised an eyebrow at her. She relented with, "I'll see you a bit later. There's a lasagna in the fridge. You only have to heat it through and make a salad when you're ready to eat."

Seth thanked his aunt one more time before returning to Cal's side.

"So, how did the Denver show go?" Cal asked him, between bites of sandwich.

"It went off okay," Seth replied, pushing aside the memory of his lackluster performance.

"Just okay?" Cal queried with a frown. "What went wrong?"

"Nothing, I... ah... just didn't play as well as I normally do, and Liam called me out on it, but to be fair, he wasn't exactly on top form either."

"Why didn't you play well? Was there something wrong?"

Seth half-smiled at Cal's baffled look. The painkillers must be messing with him because Cal was usually a lot more astute.

"Yeah, there were several things wrong."

"Like what? Dammit, I knew I should have gone back with you. I bet Jax was spitting tacks and as good as Wil is, he is still very young."

"Hey. Calm down." Seth laid a hand on Cal's shoulder, feeling the tension in his shoulders. He didn't squeeze too hard, as he didn't want to hurt him any more than he already was. "There was nothing wrong with the show, or the venue, or how Wil ran things. In fact, he did an amazing job. He really stepped up."

"So, what was wrong, then?" Cal demanded.

"Well, for starters, I spent the first twenty-four hours of married life away from my husband, and during those twenty-four hours, said husband hurts himself and ends up at the hospital. It was only the thought of disappointing all the fans that had paid to see the show—and the message from you that Art passed on—that stopped me from jumping back on the plane and flying right back to you."

Cal gaped at him. "Me? You were worried about me?"

"What kind of question is that? Of course, I was worried about you. Why wouldn't I be?"

"Because you don't really know me? I'm just a colleague. In fact, you could call me an employee and—"

Anger and hurt roared through Seth, forcing him to his feet so he could pace a few feet away from Cal. He raked a hand through his hair, biting his lip to stop the first words that wanted to spill from his mouth. Seeing Cal staring at him with wide eyes, a hint of worry in the green depths, had him taking a deep breath and then perching on the edge of the coffee table in front of the couch.

"First, you are not *just* anything. You're not *just* a colleague. You're not *just* an employee. You're not *just* the assistant helping your cousin on the tour. You are a valued crew member, and if anyone has made you feel less than that, I want their names.

"Second, I'd like to think that maybe we're friends? Maybe not best friends, but certainly a peg or two above colleagues." He paused and gripped Cal's chin gently, making him meet his gaze. "And third, do the vows you said the other night mean nothing to you? Did you not marry me and become my husband? I think that gives me every damn right to worry about you."

A faint tinge of red bloomed on Cal's cheekbones, and Seth had to fight back the urge to press his lips to the heated skin.

"I... I thought—" Cal broke off and dropped his eyes.

"You thought what, Cal?" Seth looked at him keenly as understanding dawned. "You thought that this wasn't a real marriage? That it's just a business transaction?"

The red on Cal's skin deepened, and he twisted his hands in his lap, the light catching on the gold band he wore. Seth picked up his hand and placed a butterfly kiss on the knuckle of his ring finger before brushing his thumb over the warm metal.

"I meant what I said the other night. Cal, I want this to be a real relationship. I want to get to know you better than you know yourself. I want you in my bed."

Cal gave him a skeptical look.

"What? Don't you believe me?"

"I don't know," Cal admitted with a shrug. "I mean, I believe you when you say you want me in your bed, but I don't understand why."

"Have you looked in the mirror lately? You're fuckin' hot, that's why?"

"You didn't have to marry me just to get me into your bed."

"I know that. I didn't marry you to get you into my bed. That's just an additional benefit."

"So why did you marry me, then?"

Seth blew out an exasperated breath. "You know why."

"Yeah, it was a business transaction. I needed money. You needed to meet the terms of your aunt's will. So where does worrying about me fall in all of that?" Cal gestured to Seth's left hand. "You're not even wearing your wedding band. That doesn't really strengthen your argument about this being an actual marriage."

Holding Cal's gaze, Seth reached into the neck of his t-shirt and pulled out a thin gold chain. Hanging from it was the ring Cal had clumsily slipped on his finger in Las Vegas.

"My ring hasn't left my person since you gave it to me. The only reason it's not on my finger is because we agreed to keep this quiet between us. Can you imagine how the internet would have blown up if I'd gone on stage with this on my finger? You know what our fans are like. They would have spotted it and would have kept digging until they found something out, and if they didn't find out the truth, they would have speculated and made up God only knows what. And there'd be no hiding it from the boys and the crew, either."

Seth's outburst seemed to take the wind out of Cal's sails, and he slumped back onto the couch with a resigned sigh. "Okay. Yeah, you're right. I've seen how the smallest thing can be misconstrued by the fans and media. Thank you for protecting us both."

"You're welcome." Seth took Cal's hand again, tangling their fingers together. "I like you, Cal. A lot. I care about you, and yes, I was worried about you. I'm not going to rush you into anything physical. I want to get to know you better and see how things go. Is that okay with you?"

Cal stared at him for a few seconds before giving a slow nod. "Yeah. That's okay with me. I like you too, and to be honest, if the tables had been turned, I would have been worried as well."

"So, maybe you do care about me a little?" Seth teased and grinned when a smile tugged at Cal's mouth. He picked up the pill bottle and held it out to Cal, along with the bottle of water. "Take your meds, and then we'll get you in that bath Sunny talked about."

Cal opened his mouth to protest, but at the pointed glare Seth threw his way, wisely took his meds.

Chapter Fourteen

C al lay back in the warm scented water and watched the steam tendrils snake towards the ceiling. The water was hot enough to soothe his aching muscles, but not so hot as to turn him into a cooked lobster. He fluttered his fingers, making the water quietly swish with faint ripples, and releasing the pleasant lavender scent Seth had added to the water.

He'd been surprised when Seth had opened one of the many bathroom cupboards to pull out two airtight glass jars full of coarse white powder. He'd given them both a shake to loosen the contents, and then, using a small measuring scoop put precise quantities of each into the water. Seth then pulled out a bottle of lavender essential oil and carefully poured a few drops into the bath before swirling a hand through the water to mix it all together.

"There," he'd said with a satisfied nod. "Give it another mix before you get in and then lie and soak for about fifteen minutes. Then, put the jets on for five before another five without them."

"What was that you put in the water?"

"Epsom salts, baking soda, and lavender oil. Aunt Rose used to swear by it, and it's great for relaxing your muscles. I often have a soak after a show. Helps me unwind and destress."

Cal had smirked at him. "And how often have you been stopped by TSA for containers of white powder in your luggage?"

"Once or twice," Seth admitted with a grin. "I've learned to send someone from the hotel to grab some from a local store whenever I need some. I carry a small bottle of the lavender oil with me though, because good quality stuff is hard to find."

Seth ran his eyes down Cal's body. "You know this only works if you strip and get into the water."

"Really?" Cal gave him a wide-eyed look. "I was just going to stand here and inhale the steam."

"Brat!" Seth said with a grin. "Do you need a hand with anything? I don't want you to slip and hurt yourself more."

"Thanks, I'll be fine. I promise to call you if I need help."

Seth didn't look so happy at that, but he nodded his head and pointed to the adjoining bedroom. "I'm going to have a quick shower in the guest bathroom, and then I'll just be in there. Okay?"

After Seth had left, Cal quickly stripped and sat on the edge of the bath to remove the bandage. He took a moment to admire the bruising, which was not as black today, before easing himself into the warm water.

After a few moments, his muscles relaxed, and he let his mind wander. He had to admit that a lot of the tenseness in his shoulders was more from worrying about how Seth would react on his return than from the actual fall in the kitchen.

Of course, Seth had been nothing but gentle and kind. Cal thought over their earlier conversation. With everything that had happened, he had pushed their marriage to the back of his mind, not wanting to admit that maybe Seth didn't feel the same way he did.

He lifted his hand and examined the ring on his finger. For some unknown reason, it felt and looked right. He felt Seth had been genuine when he said he cared for Cal, but the level of worry that Cal had seen in his eyes had surprised him. He was starting to realize that there was a lot more to his rockstar husband than most people saw.

He knew from being a fan for years that Seth had a bad-boy-of-rock vibe going on. One he emphasized with the tattoos, faux-hawk hairstyle, and cocky swagger when out in public. Over the last few weeks though, working behind the scenes with the band, he'd seen how much of it was a persona Seth donned to stop people from getting close. He was more relaxed and openly joked with and teased his bandmates and some of the crew when they were in private, but there was still always an air of *'stay away'* that emanated from him.

Cal mused why Seth felt the need to hide his true self. Admittedly, if he was in the public eye himself, he'd want to keep as much of life private as possible. Maybe Seth's public persona was an extension of that. Still, Cal suspected it went deeper than an innate sense of privacy.

He flicked the button on the side of the bath that activated the jets. A small groan escaped him as strategically placed pulses of water hit his aching back and shoulder muscles just right. He was tenser than he realized, and he would take Sunny's offer of her massage therapist. The gentle pummeling of the water soothed his body as he sank further into the tub's depths.

A light tap at the bathroom door interrupted his peaceful reverie, and he reluctantly opened his eyes. "Yeah?" he called out.

"You okay in there?" Seth asked.

"Um, yeah." He pushed himself upright, causing the water to slosh dangerously close to the edge of the tub.

"Do you need help to get out?"

"I think I'll be okay," he called back. "Thanks though."

There was a pause before Seth responded. "I'll stand right here. If you need help, let me know, okay? I don't want you to slip and hurt yourself even worse." When Cal didn't respond immediately, Seth called out again, his tone even more concerned than before. "Cal? Do you hear me?"

The door handle rattled, and Cal hurriedly shouted back. "I'm fine. Just... just stay there. I promise I'll call if I need you. Okay?" He knew it was silly, but he didn't want Seth to see him any more helpless than he already was. Plus, you know, the whole being naked thing.

Cal decided the safest option was to drain the tub first, so he reached down and pulled the plug. The water swirled around him as it drained away. Once most of the water had gone, he gingerly pushed himself up, using the wall to balance himself.

He figured the best way out was the same way he'd gotten in; sit on the edge of the tub and swing his feet over. That way, he didn't have to put weight on his damaged foot. He reached for one of the thick, blue towels Seth had thoughtfully left on the counter and patted himself dry. He then wrapped it around his waist and carefully lowered himself to the side of the bath.

He was halfway through the maneuver when the door burst open, startling him. With a yelp, he wobbled dangerously before warm hands landed on his biceps and steadied him.

"What are you doing? I thought I told you to call me to help you," Seth growled.

"I'm getting out of the tub, and I was perfectly fine until you burst in and scared the shit out of me!" Cal snapped back, willing his racing heart to steady. "I'm not helpless, Seth."

"I know. I'm sorry," Seth said, stepping back. "It's just that you were taking so long, and I panicked, okay? I didn't mean to frighten you."

Cal was intrigued by the dull flush that stained the usually confident rocker's face, and his heart twanged in a way it had never done before.

"Sorry for worrying you. I'm okay, and the soak has done wonders. Thank you," he said softly. "Could you maybe grab me some fresh sweats from my bag and a clean t-shirt?" he asked, hoping the small task would appease Seth.

"Sure," Seth agreed, smiling at him. "Where's your bag?"

"It's just inside your closet," Cal said.

The delighted grin that spread across Seth's face had Cal catching his breath.

"Why does that make you happy?" he called out to Seth's retreating back. He didn't get a reply, and he called out again. "Seth? Seth? What are you doing?"

Seth returned, still smiling happily, and placed the requested clothes on the counter.

"Here you go," he told him. "I'll leave you to get dressed..." he ran a speculative look up and down Cal's body, "... unless you want some help with that?"

"What? No!" Cal waved a hand at him. "Shoo! I've been dressing myself for years and having a sore foot has not diminished my capabilities."

Seth sighed and pouted. "Okay then," he said, mischief in his eyes.

Cal rolled his eyes. "I'll be out in a minute."

Once Seth had left him, not quite pulling the door fully closed behind him, Cal finished drying himself off and pulled the clothes Seth had gathered towards him. Favorite navy-blue t-shirt. Check. Comfy gray sweats. Check. Underwear... missing. He scanned the floor to see if they'd accidentally been dropped, but nothing. *Damn him*, Cal muttered and then snorted. *Fucker*. Okay then. If Seth wanted him to go commando, then commando in gray sweats, he would be.

Once he'd wriggled into his clothes and slipped the bandage back into place, he carefully hopped out of the bathroom on his crutches. He stopped short when he found Seth entering the room with a large tray loaded with food and drinks.

"Oh good, you managed okay," Seth told him, placing the tray on the bedside table. "I thought we could chill out and watch a movie or something. I grabbed some snacks and your meds." He ran a hand through his hair, making it spike in different directions. He looked... nervous? "Is that okay?"

Cal noticed the fingers of Seth's left hand twitching against his thigh. A left hand devoid of all its usual jewelry except for a wide gold band on the ring finger. Again, Cal's heart did that funny twangy-skippy thing, and he pressed a hand to his sternum.

"Yeah, sure. That sounds great, actually." He glanced at the king-sized bed. "Um, you want to do it up here rather than downstairs?"

"We could use the media room, but I thought we'd be more comfortable up here, and it means you don't have to tackle the stairs again." He rushed on. "But if you'd rather go downstairs, then, of course, we can do that."

"Actually, the thought of not having to do the stairs again is a relief. Your bed is really comfortable, so sure, we can totally chill out up here."

Cal saw some of the tension bleed out of Seth, making him wonder what Seth had been worried about.

***

Seth waited until Cal had ensconced himself on the bed before laying the tray of food next to him. He then grabbed the two spare pillows he had snagged from the guest room and offered them to Cal.

"For your foot," he said.

"Oh, thank you," Cal replied with a smile as he took them. He placed the pillows under his foot before leaning back against the headboard.

Seth felt a glow of satisfaction at the sight. Cal looked perfectly at home in his bed.

He settled himself next to Cal and picked up the remote.

"Any preferences?"

"Hmm, I haven't watched anything in months, so if there's something you want to watch, then you pick. I'm pretty easy. Just no horror or anything involving animals as the main story-line."

"What, you mean like *Lassie* or something like that?"

Cal nodded. "Yeah. I'm... I can get emotional, and trust me, you really don't need to see me ugly crying."

Seth could believe it. He'd already picked up on Cal being a natural empath, always looking out for others and feeling hurt when they hurt. His Aunt Rose had been the same. He pushed down the familiar feeling of loss that always appeared when he thought of his beloved aunt. He wondered what she would have thought of Cal and this whole situation, even if it was one of her doing. He wished too many times to count that he could ask her what she'd been thinking when she put the clause in her will. He'd already been successful when she'd made her final will, just after being diagnosed, and knew that he wouldn't need the money.

Of course, she knew that he wouldn't want his father to get anything that was meant for him. She'd encouraged and enabled his rebellious behavior as a teenager, but making marriage the condition of inheriting, it still didn't compute. Even her own sister had thought it very odd.

"Okay then. Good to know," he said, turning his attention to the screen. "I've been wanting to catch up on the latest Marvel movie. Have you seen any of them?"

"Yes," Cal said, drawing the word out, causing Seth to flick his gaze and catching a flood of red staining Cal's pale skin.

"Hmm. From the red face, I'm picking you've got a favorite character or two?"

"I will neither confirm nor deny that I may have read one or two Stucky fanfics," Cal said, skin turning an even deeper shade of red, even as his eyes sparkled in amusement.

"Stucky?"

"Yeah, y'know. Steve and Bucky. Stucky." Cal gave him a sly grin. "Have you not heard of Stucky?"

Seth opened his mouth to reply as his brain supplied images of the very buff Captain America and the equally buff bad-boy Winter Soldier. "No, I've not. And now I'm going to need links to said fan fics, please and thank you."

Cal snorted in delight next to him. "Sure thing." He nodded to the TV. "So, latest movie, or do we rewatch Winter Soldier?"

"Latest movie. I need to catch up before we hit the road again, otherwise, Jamie will spoil it for me."

"He's a fan too?"

"Yeah," Seth answered as he got the movie playing. "We all are. Though, I don't know about Kellet. If he's not, he soon will be. We've had days-long marathons watching them all in chronological order."

Cal gave a low whistle as he shuffled down the bed, rearranging his pillows. "That is some commitment. Count me in for the next one."

Pleasure washed through Seth at the thought. He liked the idea of Cal being around long enough for the next time the band did their big movie night.

He nudged Cal's elbow and nodded to the tray between them. "Take your meds and have something to eat."

Cal nodded and did as he was told as they settled in to watch the opening credits.

CHAPTER FIFTEEN

S eth meandered along the partially hidden path that ran from his art studio to the house, ducking under the low-hanging branches of the shade trees he'd planted. The temperature was slowly cooling from the low eighties it had been all day. Fortunately, his studio had air conditioning, so he'd been comfortable as he'd sketched and painted for most of the day.

It was part of his ritual when returning home from a tour or an extended stay away from home. It helped center him after the hustle and bustle of performing. He loved his job, but he loved the peace his art brought him too.

His head was still full of the images he'd captured this morning. Almost of their own volition, his hands had sketched a slumbering Cal. He cast his mind back to their evening the night before. They'd watched the movie while snacking and making general conversation about their favorite parts of the Marvel Universe. As the evening wore on, Cal had slipped further down the bed and had drifted off to sleep as soon as the end credits started rolling.

Seth had used an incredible amount of restraint to stop himself from gathering the man up in his arms. He'd almost dropped the tray when Cal had come out of the bedroom in the gray sweats and tight navy t-shirt. The sweats had clung to his damp skin, emphasizing his bubble butt, and as Seth had accidentally, on purpose, forgotten to take underwear in, the definite bulge in the front of his pants.

He'd had a fitful night's sleep, trying not to roll into Cal and take him in his arms. Of course, when Cal had rolled *into him*, he'd tucked the smaller man in close and finally fallen into a deeper sleep.

He was nearing the house when his aunt called out to him.

"Seth Joseph Worthington, where have you been?"

He stopped dead in his tracks, frozen by the irritated tone he rarely heard from his usually chilled-out aunt.

"In my studio. You know I always head there to decompress when I'm home."

"Uh huh," she replied, glaring at him, her arms crossed. "And I suppose you lost yourself in your drawing and completely forgot about the outside world?"

"Ah, yeah, I guess I did," he admitted sheepishly. "Why? Did you need me for something?"

"Did *I* need you for something?" Sunny closed her eyes and took a deep breath as if gathering the patience to deal with him. Again, something she rarely did. Brown eyes shot daggers at him, and he almost took a step backwards. "*Did I need you for something?*" she ground out.

He wisely said nothing, realizing that anything he said would probably send her nuclear.

"No. *I* did not need you for anything. But *your husband* may have liked to, oh, I don't know, spend some time with you. Know where you were. How long you were going to be. Just minor details like that."

Seth's stomach dropped. *Oh shit.* Cal. He'd left him sleeping this morning. He hadn't even left him a note. He must have felt abandoned.

"Fuck!" he said succinctly.

"Indeed," his aunt agreed. "I suggest you hightail it inside and start making amends. That poor boy has been rattled from pillar to post this week and deserves to be treated better."

Shame flooded through Seth at the disappointment in Sunny's voice, and he nodded in agreement. "You're right. Dammit, I've fucked up. I lost track of time...." He stopped as Sunny held up a hand, which she then used to point to the house.

Right. Don't make excuses. Deal with the issue. Something he learned from his parents, and while he might not get along with them, it was one of the life lessons he tried to live by.

As he passed Sunny, he paused and pressed a kiss to her cheek. "I'm sorry."

"I know you are, Seth. But it's not me you have to apologize to. I've known you from the day you were born. I know you. I know you didn't do it deliberately. That man in there has only known you for a few months." She tilted her head at him. "Does he know about your art?"

"No," Seth replied with a shake of his head. "You know I don't share it with many people."

"Well, you really need to share it with your husband, don't you think?"

With another nod and a sigh, he continued up the path to the house.

Entering through the kitchen door, he paused and took a breath, sorting through the words he needed—and wanted—to say. He spied movement over the top of the couch, Cal's blond hair shining in the late afternoon sun.

He was about to call out when he heard a loud sniff. And then another. A muttered curse and a choked back sob had him striding quickly into the den.

"Cal? What's wrong? Are you in pain?" he asked, rounding the end of the couch. Cal was hunched up, a large gray t-shirt swamping him.

Cal jumped when he saw Seth, and hastily used the edge of his shirt to wipe his eyes and nose.

"Seth," he said, voice cracking. "I... I didn't hear you come in."

"What's happened?" Seth dropped beside him on the couch, hands hovering, unsure if he could or should touch him.

Cal leaned away, and Seth felt a stab of rejection at the movement. Not that he didn't deserve it. Christ, he'd sat here yesterday and told Cal he wanted to get to know him better than he knew himself. Wanted to be a husband in every sense of the word, and what had he done? Disappeared on their first day together.

"I'm so sorry I left you all day," he rushed out. "I got caught up and didn't realize the time, and I'm so, so sorry. I didn't mean to upset you."

Cal sniffed again, and Seth reached over to the end table for the small box of tissues that Sunny had put there. He'd never understood why he needed tissues on his end table, but right now, he was grateful for them.

Cal gave him a watery smile of thanks and took a handful. After wiping his eyes and blowing his nose, he tucked the used tissues into the pocket of his shorts.

"Are you okay now?" Seth asked.

"Yes. Sorry, you had to see that, but I did warn you I was an ugly crier."

"What upset you? I promise. I didn't mean to abandon you all day."

"You're going to think I'm stupid," Cal said, red tinging his cheeks.

"No. I'm not. Please, tell me."

Cal waved his phone at him.

"Did you get bad news? Is it your family?"

Cal snorted a laugh. "No. I was watching TikTok videos. In particular, the 'coming home' videos. Y'know, where a military spouse or family member returns to surprise their loved ones. Some of them are just so heart-warming."

"And they make you cry?" Seth asked, a little unsure.

"Yes. See, I told you it was stupid. What grown man cries just because someone he doesn't know is surprising his wife?"

"Oh, Cal," Seth breathed as he pulled him in for a hug. "You are the most adorable, wonderfully kind-hearted person I know. It's not stupid at all."

Cal was stiff in his arms, and Seth stroked a hand up and down his spine, trying to relax him. He inhaled Cal's scent of sunshine and lemons, and Seth could have held him all day. Cal pulled back though, and Seth reluctantly let him go.

"I'm not usually that bad," he admitted. "I guess everything just hit me, and it was a bit of stress relief."

Seth felt bad again. He was contributing to that stress.

"Why don't I get us something to eat, and we can sit and maybe watch another movie or something?"

Cal shook his head. "No. Thanks, but I'm not in the mood for a movie tonight."

"What would you like to do?"

"Don't worry about me," Cal said with a wave of his hand. "You can carry on with whatever plans you have. I don't want to interrupt your routines or anything." Cal's tone was a touch sarcastic, and Seth gave an internal wince.

"I don't have any plans, and if I did, you wouldn't be interrupting them at all."

Cal raised a skeptical brow at him, and Seth felt himself flush. Damn, it had been a long time since someone had made him feel like a disappointment. His parents didn't count, as he had long learned to ignore anything they said or did.

"I'm sorry. You're right. I'm not very good at thinking about someone else. I'm usually here on my own, and I didn't mean to ignore you all day."

***

Cal eyed the man he'd married. He knew he shouldn't have done it. He knew he should have just slept with Seth, got him out of his system, and figured out a way to pay off his debt. Seth seemed genuinely apologetic. He wasn't making up excuses, but on the other hand, neither was he being overly forthcoming about where he'd been all day.

Cal had woken up expecting to spend the day with Seth. Getting to know the man better. They'd had a good time last night. At least, Cal thought they had. He'd enjoyed watching the movie with a fellow fan, and looked forward to introducing Seth to the rabbit hole that was Stucky fanfiction.

When he'd woken up alone, he'd presumed Seth had got up for a run or something—not that he knew if Seth had a fitness routine—and had expected to find him in the kitchen. But no. It hadn't taken Cal long to realize that Seth wasn't anywhere in the house.

He'd spent most of the day rattling around the large house. He was so bored. He didn't miss the stress of working sixty-hour weeks for a gaming company or the hustle and bustle of the tour, but he did miss the motivation of having something to do.

He'd done some laundry and then pottered about in the kitchen. He'd thought about preparing dinner but had no idea what Seth liked to eat, so in the end, he made up some healthy snacks that he could graze on. He'd then lost himself in the time-suck that was TikTok. Ten-second videos that make you lose hours of your life.

And, of course, Seth had returned just as he'd got to a really sappy montage of videos. He hadn't lied before. Most of the tears had been pent-up stress, but he didn't really feel much better. Just tired. Tired of being broke. Tired of not having any direction. Tired of being a burden on people. Tired of life.

"What are you thinking, Cal?" Seth asked quietly.

"Sorry. Having a pity party for one." He tried smiling, but it felt more like a grimace. "You go ahead. I might take another bath and see if that helps relax me a bit."

"No."

"No?" Cal blinked at Seth in surprise. He really hadn't expected the man to deny him a bath.

"No. Where are your crutches? I want to show you what I've been doing all day."

"You don't have to—"

Cal was cut off by Seth, standing and reaching for the set of crutches that were lying on the floor at the end of the couch. "Yes. I do. As Aunt Sunny reminded me, you're my husband, and you need to know about me and what I do when I get home from tour."

Cal took Seth's proffered hand, his gaze once again snagging on the gold band as he was gently pulled upright. Settling into his crutches, he nodded at Seth. "Lay on, Macduff."

"Shakespeare fan, huh?"

"No. Definitely not. We did Macbeth at school, and it's one phrase that I remember, other than the witches opening scene and, of course, '*out damn spot*'."

Seth chuckled. "Come on. Just go at your own pace. We're not going far. Just to the end of the garden."

Cal balanced himself on his crutches and slowly followed Seth outside. He was led down a path he hadn't noticed before—not that he'd had the chance to do any exploring—and gingerly swung himself along the rough-hewn path. Seth didn't explain where they were going, just murmuring a warning every now and again, pointing out an exposed tree root or particularly rough section of path.

"How big is the property?" Cal asked.

"Useable land, not that much," Seth replied. "The property line is just before the edge of the canyon. There was just enough space for me to build my studio at the boundary."

A small white stucco building came into view, the late afternoon sun casting shadows and bathing it in a warm glow.

"I thought your studio was in the house?" Cal queried; he was sure he'd heard Seth mention it before.

"The recording studio is, yes." He nodded to the building as they reached the door. "This is my art studio."

Cal stopped and stared at Seth, fascinated by the way he wouldn't quite meet Cal's gaze.

"Art studio? You paint?"

"A little, yes. I prefer charcoal and soft, medium materials." He opened the door and ushered Cal ahead of him.

Cal hitched his way into the large open space. The far wall was all windows, currently covered by pull-down blinds, keeping out the glare of the setting sun. There were several easels of different sizes placed in the corner. The wall nearest him had a small sink and refrigerator, a large cupboard, and a shelving unit stacked with canvases and art pads of different sizes. A door led off to one side, which Cal presumed was a bathroom.

"Come and sit down," Seth said, directing him towards the large faded blue couch near the windows.

As Cal got himself comfortable, Seth pressed a button on the wall, and there was a quiet whir of a motor as the blinds lifted, unveiling a spectacular view across Cold Water Canyon.

"Wow," Cal gasped.

Seth gave him a shy smile before moving towards a drawer unit Cal hadn't spotted before. It was about hip height, made of wood that shone in the warm light. There were several papers neatly stacked on the top, and Seth shuffled through them, his touch gentle and reverent.

He paused, worrying his bottom lip in a nervous gesture that sent a pang of feeling through Cal. He realized with sudden insight that this was something that Seth didn't share with everyone. He caught a flash of blue eyes as Seth glanced over his shoulder and saw the way he steeled himself before turning to Cal with that shy smile again.

"Um. I like to sketch and sometimes paint to help me decompress." He thrust the papers towards Cal, who took them gently, keeping his fingers to the edges so as not to smudge or mark the delicate work.

He rested the sheets on his lap and slowly took in the dark sweeps and curves that captured the view of the valley below perfectly. Predominantly black and white, Seth had highlighted certain areas with faint splashes of gold and green, adding a depth to the drawing that drew the eye in and held it.

"Oh, Seth. This is gorgeous." He smiled up at the man hovering a few feet away. "The pictures in the hallway, back in the house. They're all yours, aren't they?"

Seth nodded. "Most of them are. There are a couple by Aunt Rose. She's the one that encouraged and supported my art."

"Do you have any formal training?" Cal asked as he gently laid the first picture to one side to reveal a fun sketch of the band rehearsing. He'd captured Liam's serious face but had tempered it with a stray curl on his forehead. Jamie was leaning back with the microphone close to his mouth in an exaggerated rock star pose. Kellet was drawn with a drumstick twirling between his fingers, a grin on his face, happiness radiating off him.

Cal grinned. "I love this one. You've caught the guys perfectly."

Seth dropped beside him on the couch. "Yeah, Kellet took a few goes to get right, as it's been a while since I've drawn him, but I can almost draw Jamie and Liam in my sleep."

"So you've always drawn, even as a teenager?" Cal asked.

"I think I got my first art set from Aunt Rose when I was five or six. She loved art in all its forms and tried to expose my brother and me to it as much as possible." He snorted. "Of course, my parents weren't so keen as we got older, feeling art and music were frivolous pursuits. Something to be looked at and admired from a distance once or twice a year when networking for business. And certainly not something a son of theirs should pursue as a career."

Cal heard the bitterness in Seth's tone, and he laid a hand on his arm. "I'm sorry they felt that way. You're very talented in both your music and art. Do they still feel the same?"

"Yep," Seth said, popping the 'p'. "But I learned a long time ago not to let it get to me. They're entitled to their opinions, and I don't need their approval."

He may not need their approval, but Cal would bet everything he owned that some part of Seth still wanted it.

"Is that why you're so close to your aunts?"

"Yeah. Aunt Rose married very well and could indulge her passion. Aunt Sunny is more holistic than arty. She and her ex-husband founded and set up a wellness retreat that basically runs itself these days. She has a great team running it, and she goes in a few days a week and hangs out. Most of the guests think she's either one of them or one of the instructors. She never lets on that she's the owner."

"So when she suggested her masseur, she meant one of her staff?"

"Yes. I've used them a time or two. Another of my post-tour rituals. We should go up there tomorrow and have a spa day. It will do us both a world of good."

Cal murmured his agreement as he looked back down at the pictures in his lap. He moved the one of the band to the side and froze as his own face stared up at him.

Seth had captured him sleeping, his profile in repose, bottom lip soft and relaxed. His hair was sticking up in several places, and his lashes lay in a dark shadow against his cheek. His left hand with his wedding band was curled under his chin.

His gaze flew up to Seth's. "When....?"

"I drew it this morning. You looked so peaceful and relaxed."

Cal traced a finger above the line of his shoulder that showed above the crumpled sheet. "I didn't hear you."

"I... ah... drew it from memory."

At Seth's admission, Cal stared at him. "From memory?"

"I know it sounds creepy," Seth rushed to explain. "I promise, I haven't been watching you sleep. Honest. I have a semi-photographic memory."

Cal gaped at the man he married. Talk about hidden depths.

"I'm flattered," he said, returning his gaze to the picture. Wanting to break the tension a little, he nudged Seth's arm. "But did you have to draw me with bed head? Really?"

Seth grinned, tugging the picture out of his hands. "It's cute. I like it." He nudged Cal back. "Just be grateful I didn't add in the drool."

Cal gasped and raised a hand as if to wipe his chin, and Seth laughed. He reached out and brushed Cal's bottom lip.

"There's no drool, I promise," he said huskily.

Cal swiped his tongue along his lip, and Seth sucked in a breath. Heat flared in Cal's veins, and his eyes dipped to Seth's lips before rising to meet his heated gaze. The air thickened between them, and Cal suddenly wanted nothing more than the man in front of him.

"Cal?" Seth whispered.

Cal nodded and gave his own sigh as Seth's mouth met his.

CHAPTER SIXTEEN

S eth gently brushed his lips against Cal's, wanting to capture their fullness. He slowly applied pressure, not wanting to push Cal any further than he was willing to go. Cal responded by tilting his head and snaking a hand around Seth's neck to pull him closer. With the next brush of his lips, Cal opened for him, and with a soft groan, he sank deeper into the kiss, taking in the taste of his husband.

He took his time, wanting to savor the moment. They'd only had two brief kisses, and neither one had been enough for Seth. Strong fingers carded through his hair as Cal tugged him closer, and together they fell back onto the couch. Seth gripped Cal's hips to swivel him round so he could get him beneath him when Cal winced and froze.

Shit! His foot. He pulled away, scanning Cal's lithe body. "Are you okay?"

"I'm fine. Sorry." Cal apologized, and Seth reached over to trace a finger down his cheek before gently clasping his chin.

"Don't apologize. It was my fault. I wasn't thinking. Seems to be the theme of the day," he said ruefully.

"I'm fine, honestly," Cal reassured him. "I'm probably due for some painkillers."

Seth helped him to his feet, hands resting on his hips as he steadied himself. Cal gave him a pointed look when he didn't move away.

"Just making sure you're not going to fall over and hurt yourself."

Cal grinned and brushed a quick kiss across his mouth before rolling his eyes, and Seth chuckled as he moved away, letting Cal go ahead of him. He lowered the blinds and returned the drawings to the cabinet as Cal waited for him by the door.

They made their way back to the house, and Seth made sure Cal was comfortable before heading into the kitchen to grab them both a bottle of water. He checked the fridge to see what they could have for dinner, but nothing really appealed, and besides, he wasn't in the mood to cook.

"Want to order in?" he called out.

"Any good pizza places around here?"

"Yeah. There's a really good one not too far away that delivers," Seth told him as he returned with their water. He pulled out his phone and pulled up the ordering app. "What do you like?"

"I could really go for a deep-dish pepperoni," Cal said.

Seth nodded and sent the order. He got a confirmation chime back in a few seconds. "All ordered. Should be here in about twenty minutes."

"Your art is amazing, Seth. Thank you for sharing it with me."

The softly spoken compliment hit Seth like an arrow, piercing through a layer of the armor he had placed around himself. He wasn't sure how to react. Not many people saw what he did. The guys knew he drew, and they all had pieces in their homes, but the sincerity in Cal's tone touched a part of him that hadn't been touched since Aunt Rose died.

"Thank you. I don't share it with many people."

"So you've never done a show at a gallery or anything?"

"Fuck no! I'm not that good," Seth retorted, horrified at the thought.

"You are, and I dare anyone to say that you're not in my hearing," Cal told him, green eyes stormy.

Another arrow hit Seth. *Dammit! This man was getting under his skin.* It had been a long time since anyone other than his aunts or his brother had stood up for him.

"Thank you, Cal. That means a lot to me. But my art is for me. I share just about every other aspect of my life with thousands of fans all over the world. They have my music, but my art, my drawings, they're for me."

Cal looked contrite at Seth's words and nodded slowly.

"Sorry. I can understand that. You're right." He gave Seth a shy smile. "I feel honored that you've shared it with me."

"Do you have any hobbies?" Seth asked, wanting to move the attention away from himself.

Cal either didn't notice or decided to ignore the deflection, because he shrugged. "Sort of. I mean, I love my job coding and creating gaming software. I just don't love the hours and the politics involved. It takes up so much of my time that any downtime I have, I tend to just blob on the couch, watching a movie or TV show." He shrugged. "Sorry, I'm pretty boring."

"Cal, you're anything but boring." Seth's phone chimed before he could say anything else. "Dinner's here. Choose something to watch while we eat," he said, tossing the remote to Cal.

***

An hour later, they were replete from their meal of pizza and chuckling as they watched *Schitt's Creek*.

Cal was glad he'd seen this episode several times because his attention kept being dragged away by Seth. His guard was completely down, laugh lines crinkling around his eyes. Cal was still a little overwhelmed by the fact that Seth had shared his art with him, and how amazingly talented he was. It added another layer of attraction to the complex man, and Cal wanted to explore each layer intimately.

"Do I have something on my face?" Seth asked, making Cal startle and realize that he'd been staring.

"No, sorry. Miles away."

"Anything you want to talk about?" Seth offered.

Rather than bring up Seth's art again, Cal shrugged. "Just wondering what I'm going to do once things are sorted out with Systems Corp."

"Do about what?" Seth asked with a frown. Cal resisted the urge to lean over and smooth out his furrowed brow.

Instead, he picked at an invisible piece of lint on his pants. "I'm bored, Seth." He glanced up as Seth turned off the television and swiveled towards him. "I mean, I'm used to being busy. Too busy, in fact, and now I've got nothing to do."

"Has Jax not got anything for you?"

"No, not really. I spoke to her when I hurt my foot, and she said not to worry about anything for the tour as it was all organized and she'd let me know if she needed my help." He gestured to his foot. "And besides, this isn't going to be fixed in a week. How helpful am I going to be on the tour if I'm hobbling around?"

"There'll be stuff you can do, I'm sure," Seth said. "We can set you up at the arena, and then Wil can run around and do all the things you can't."

Cal shook his head. "No. Wil has his own responsibilities, and it's not fair to rearrange everything just because I'm not mobile. And it's not just for the tour. What am I going to do once it's finished? I need to find a job. One I'm qualified for."

"Well, technically, you don't need to work. As my husband, you can become a gentleman of leisure."

Cal gave him a flat look. "I'm not leeching off you, Seth. I've told you I don't want anything from you other than the loan. I need to pay my own way, and that means having a job."

Seth tangled their fingers together, sending tendrils of warmth through Cal. "Okay. I can appreciate that."

"Why do I feel there's a but coming?"

"But," Seth said with a grin, "I think it's something we can discuss tomorrow. It's still going to be a problem tomorrow, and I feel we'll be able to brainstorm better after a good night's sleep."

Sleep? Cal highly doubted he'd get much of that with Seth laying next to him. Not after the kiss they'd shared in the art studio. A kiss that he wanted to take further. It had been so long since he'd been with anyone and being around Seth the last few months had only pushed his feelings from crush to full on attraction. He wanted Seth. Badly.

"Cal?"

"Hmm?"

"What do you think?"

"Think?" Cal blinked back to awareness and felt heat flood his face. Dammit. He'd drifted off again. He took in Seth's concerned gaze and gave in to temptation. Leaning forward, he rested a hand on Seth's shoulder. "I think we should pick up where we left off earlier."

He had a second to take in Seth's confused expression before their mouths met. Seth opened for him immediately, returning his kiss for a few seconds before pulling away.

"Are you sure?" Seth asked, his eyes searching Cal's face. "Because if we start something now, I'm not sure I can stop until I'm inside you."

Desire shot through Cal like a Californian wildfire, heating his blood and sending it south. He nodded. "Yes. Please."

Seth's eyes darkened with his own desire. He stood, gently pulling Cal to his feet. "Bedroom. Now."

CHAPTER SEVENTEEN

S eth pushed his bedroom door closed, eyes tracking Cal as the other man made his way to the bed. Cal hesitated, uncertainty clear on his face as he worried his bottom lip with his teeth.

"Cal, we don't have to do this if you're having second thoughts."

"No, I'm not having second thoughts," Cal replied, and then sighed when Seth raised a skeptical eyebrow. "I'm not, I'm just... nervous, I guess."

Seth didn't like that and crossed the room to stand in front of him. "Is there something I can say or do to ease your nerves? I promise, we won't do anything you don't want to do. If you'd rather just cuddle and make out, then I'm good with that."

Cal smiled and rested a hand on Seth's chest, its warmth a gentle weight that grounded Seth. "Thanks. Maybe we start with that. I'm feeling a little less sexy, what with these and all," he said, gesturing to the crutches leaning against the bed next to them.

"Oh, baby. You could be in full body armor, and you'd still be as sexy as hell. A couple of metal poles aren't going to change that." He gently pushed Cal to sit on the side of the bed. "You sit there and leave everything to me."

He moved the crutches to what had become Cal's side of the bed, before returning to kneel in front of his husband. Placing a hand on either side of Cal's slim hips, he leaned forward and pressed small butterfly kisses up Cal's throat, the skin warm and silky beneath his lips. A fine tremor ran through Cal, goose-bumps raising on his skin.

He nibbled along Cal's jawline, feeling the faint scrub of stubble, too fair to see, before flicking his tongue over his ear-lobe, followed by a gentle bite. A low moan rumbled from Cal as he pressed a warm hand to Seth's nape, his other tangling in Seth's t-shirt. With a firm grip, Cal pulled him closer, arching his neck to the side to give Seth more room.

"Feel good, baby?" Seth said huskily.

"Mmm hmm," Cal whimpered, leaning back and tugging Seth up so he could kiss him. Seth let Cal take the lead, allowing him to explore his mouth, the kiss slowly deepening. Fire licked along Seth's veins. He wanted to feel and taste all of Cal. Reluctantly breaking their kiss, he rested their foreheads together.

"Why don't we lie down properly and get comfortable? I'm less likely to hurt your foot if I don't have to manhandle you."

Cal nodded, his eyes dark and skin flushed. Seth wondered how far down his body that flush went, and in the hope of encouraging Cal to remove his shirt, Seth tugged his own off over his head.

From his position against the pillows, Cal eyed him like he was his favorite dessert he was about to indulge in. Seth wasn't vain—well, no more than any other red-blooded male that was in the public eye with a huge fan base—but he took pride in his body, and it felt good to see someone appreciate what he had to offer.

"Seth?"

"Yeah," Seth replied as he eased over Cal, keeping his weight on his elbows and knees.

"When my foot's healed, will you manhandle me then?"

It took Seth a second to figure out what Cal was asking. When he did, a burst of pleasure and anticipation shot through him. "Oh, do you like it a bit rough, Mr. Stevens?"

"No, not so much rough. I just like it when my partner isn't afraid to move me around." Cal hesitated, and Seth nudged his nose with his own, encouraging him to go on. "And... and to let me move them around."

"Are you versatile?" Seth asked, not wanting to assume.

"Yeah. Most people think I'm a dedicated bottom, thanks to looking like a twenty-year-old twink, and I do tend to bottom more than top, but I do like to change it up every now and again." He bit his lip, uncertainty playing across his face. "Is... is that okay with you?"

Seth's dick pushed against his zipper at the thought of Cal topping him. He rolled his hips against Cal's thigh. "Does this tell you what I think of that?" he growled.

Cal gasped, his hand landing on Seth's jeans-clad ass and pulling him closer. "You're vers too?"

"I am, but I top more than anything, but I'm not averse to bottoming with the right person."

Cal gave him a sexy smile, one that lit up his face, his eyes bright with desire and want.

"And while we're having this discussion, now would be a good time to mention that I'm negative. We all get tested at the beginning of the tour, and I haven't been with anyone since before then, so I'm all good in that department."

Cal's eyes widened in shock. "You mean to say you haven't had sex with anyone for five months?"

"Actually, closer to six months. I think the last time was—" He broke off. "Actually, this is neither the time nor the place to talk about that. Suffice to say, you are the only person I've been interested in, so no, there hasn't been anyone else since rehearsals started."

"Well, I'm not sure how to respond to that, other than to say I also tested negative at the beginning of the tour, and as I haven't been with anyone in over a year, I'm almost a born-again virgin."

Seth snorted and ran a hand down Cal's side, tugging at his t-shirt. "Good to know. Wanna remove this, so we can be more comfortable?"

Cal pulled his shirt off, and Seth lay beside him, watching as the pink flush that stained his face slowly tracked down Cal's neck and shoulders. Seth ran a finger along Cal's collarbone, down his chest, before delicately tracing around his small brown nipple.

Goosebumps pebbled Cal's skin and the nub under his finger hardened to stand proud. Seth carried on down Cal's rib cage to his waist. Cal sucked in a breath and flinched slightly under Seth's delicate touch, and Seth smiled at the response.

"Ticklish?"

"May... maybe," Cal squeaked out as Seth did it again, this time adding a little extra pressure.

"I promise not to torment you too much," Seth told him, before lowering his head, following the same path his finger had taken with his tongue and lips. He feathered delicate kisses along Cal's collarbone, and then his tongue teased his nipple, making Cal arch and card his fingers through Seth's hair to pull him closer.

He smiled against Cal's skin, before nibbling along his rib cage and across his soft, flat belly to press a kiss to his belly button. He then repeated everything up the other side of Cal's smooth torso until he got to Cal's right ear. Beneath him, Cal was quivering, his breath coming in sharp pants.

"You okay?"

A hand scrabbled for his, tugging it until it landed on the soft material of Cal's sweats. Sweats that were tented by a steel hardness pushing against Seth's hand. Seth groaned and took the invitation offered. He gently squeezed, feeling the sizeable length beneath his palm jerk. His own cock jerked in response, and Seth needed to see and taste all of Cal.

He pushed to his knees and tugged at Cal's sweats and underwear. Cal obliged, lifting his hips so Seth could pull the material away. He carefully eased them over Cal's injured left foot before tossing them off the end of the bed.

He looked over Cal's pale body. His skin was rosy with the flush of desire. He had no chest hair, but there was the very faint fuzz of a treasure trail leading to pale trimmed curls nestling around a tight set of balls and a leaking, rosy cock.

"Fuck, Cal, you're even more gorgeous than I imagined," he ground out, his hand reaching for the button on his jeans. He needed to feel all of that skin against his own.

"Can I?" Cal asked, his hand hovering over Seth's.

"Do whatever you want to me, baby," Seth told him, edging forward so Cal could unzip his jeans. Cal ran a hand down Seth's abs before tracing the hardness that pushed against the zipper. He slowly tugged the tab down, and Seth's cock pushed forward, happy to be released from its confines. Cal ran his fingers up the shaft enclosed in the soft cotton of his boxer briefs, and Seth's hips nudged forward of their own volition.

"Off," Cal muttered, tugging at the denim. Seth hopped off the bed and quickly shed the rest of his clothes.

"I wanna taste you," Cal whispered, his eyes flicking between Seth's face and his cock, which was standing proudly against his stomach.

Seth knee-walked over the bed until he was next to Cal's face. He held himself still as Cal traced a delicate finger up his shaft before rubbing the pad of his thumb over the crown, swiping through the bead of precum that pearled at the tip. Eyes fixed on Seth's, Cal sucked the moisture off his thumb. Seth grasped the base of his cock, the pinch of pain making his orgasm recede.

Cal leaned up on his elbow, leaning over in to guide Seth's straining cock to his mouth. Again, keeping eye contact, he sucked the tip into his mouth, swirling his tongue over the slit and down around the sensitive crown.

"Fuck, Cal. So good, baby," Seth huffed out, brushing Cal's hair off his forehead to get a better view of his eyes, so dark with desire. Cal popped off and stroked a hand down Seth's shaft, spreading precum and saliva, before taking him back into the warm cavern of his mouth. He sucked while jacking the base of Seth's cock.

Seth reached between Cal's legs and took Cal's dick into his hand, mimicking the strokes that Cal was administering to his own cock. Cal whimpered around Seth's cock, sending a bolt of heat through Seth.

He pulled out of Cal's mouth, leaning down to capture the slick, swollen lips in a deep kiss. He could faintly taste himself on Cal's tongue.

"My turn," he murmured against Cal's lips before sliding down the bed to lie between Cal's thighs. Cal shifted on the bed, spreading his legs wider to accommodate Seth's shoulders.

Seth rolled Cal's balls in his hand, the skin warm and soft. He ran his tongue up the straining shaft before placing a butterfly kiss on the tip. Cal grunted impatiently, nudging his hips up.

"Want something, baby?" Seth teased, his fingers still tracing around Cal's balls, occasionally dipping lower to fondle the soft skin of his taint.

"Seth," Cal whined. "Stop teasing and suck me. Please."

"Seeing as you asked so nicely," Seth replied before taking Cal into his mouth. Salty flavor burst across his tongue as precum spurted from Cal's dick. Seth hummed at the taste, hollowing his cheeks as he sucked. He inched down Cal's shaft until he felt the tip nudge the back of his throat. He pulled back up and repeated the process until Cal was fucking his mouth.

He felt Cal's balls tighten, and with a final hard suck, he pulled off. Cal whimpered in protest.

"Shh. I'm just getting the lube," Seth soothed him, leaning across the bed to the bedside table. He retrieved the lube and a condom, dropping them both on the bed before laying his body over Cal's. Cal wrapped his arms around Seth's shoulders as their mouths met in a deep kiss. Their lower bodies rocked together, both seeking the friction to ease their aching cocks.

"I'm gonna come if you keep doing that," Cal said breathlessly. "I wanna feel you inside me, Seth."

"You sure?" Seth asked.

"Yes. Please."

Seth reached for the condom, ripping the packet open.

"Can I put that on you?" Cal asked, stretching out a hand. Seth dropped the latex into Cal's palm. He'd never had a partner do this before. He gasped as Cal's delicate fingers slowly rolled the condom down his cock, teasing him as he went.

"Fuck!" he ground out, grabbing his balls and tugging them sharply. "That's so fuckin' erotic."

Reaching for the lube, Seth quickly squirted some onto his fingers, wanting to be inside Cal. He ran a finger around Cal's hole a few times before gently pushing inside. Cal moaned, the sound shooting straight to Seth's balls. He dribbled more lube over Cal's hole before adding a second finger.

Cal writhed under him as Seth scissored his fingers, loosening the tight muscles. Despite his urgency to be inside his husband, he was determined to make sure Cal was as ready as he could be, especially since he hadn't been with anyone in a while.

"Seth, please. I need you."

"Shh, baby. Nearly there," Seth crooned, adding a third finger. "I don't want to hurt you." He leaned forward and kissed Cal deeply.

"You won't. Please. Now." Cal's hand stroked Seth's aching cock. "Pass me the lube."

Seth grabbed the bottle and poured a little onto Cal's hand. Cal slowly jacked him, spreading the lube over the condom, before moving his hand to his own cock to spread what was left on his own.

"You're so damn sexy," Seth told him as he positioned himself between Cal's thighs.

"Not so bad yourself," Cal replied, his breath hitching as Seth guided his cock to notch against his hole.

Balancing his weight on his elbows, Seth kissed Cal as he slowly pushed his hips forward. Cal tensed beneath him but prevented Seth from pulling away by running his hands down Seth's back to clasp his ass. Seth paused, waiting for the muscles to relax. After a moment, Cal gave him a nod, and Seth inched forward again.

"Oh shit. That feels so good," Cal whimpered.

"You should feel it from this side. You're so damn tight, baby."

Cal leaned up to kiss up Seth's neck. Warm breath tickled against his ear as Cal whispered, "Move, Seth."

Seth rocked slowly, wanting to savor every second of being enveloped in the tight, hot channel. His thrusts got longer, drawing back until he was almost pulling out of Cal's body and then sliding all the way back in, pushing as far as he could until his balls were slapping against Cal's.

Beneath him, Cal gasped and rocked his pelvis to meet Seth.

"More, Seth," Cal moaned.

Seth pushed up onto his knees, gently lifting Cal's left leg so his ankle rested on his right shoulder. The change in angle had Cal arching his back and reaching for his cock, which was leaking on to his stomach.

Seth reached down and swiped at the pre-cum, licking his thumb as Cal watched him with hooded eyes.

"You taste so sweet, baby," Seth told him.

Cal bit his lip, jacking himself faster as he chased his release. His skin glowed like a pearl, a fine sheen of sweat across his chest.

The sight made Seth's blood heat, and sparks danced along his lower back and into his balls.

"Not going to... *fuck*... last long," he ground out as he pounded into Cal.

"Ahh, don't stop. Please, Seth." Cal was a whimpering mess, his body tensing and twitching as he rode Seth's cock, his hand shuttling faster on his own. "Oh. Oh. Shit. Seth!" Cal's orgasm ripped through him, his free hand grasping at Seth's wrist where it lay on his hip, nails scratching at his skin. Cum spurted on his belly, his cock flushed and red as he stroked himself to completion.

Seth lowered Cal's leg so he could arch over him and push into him faster and harder, his weight on his hands as he drove in and out. The clench of Cal's ass around his dick was the sweetest vice Seth could imagine.

Hands landed on his hips, urging him on. "Yes, Seth. You feel so good. Don't stop. Come for me."

Cal's words in his ear sent Seth over the ledge, and he came with a grunt. He dropped to cover Cal, hips still rutting as he filled the condom.

Slowly, his body relaxed, and his breathing slowed to normal. He pressed a kiss to Cal's damp neck, inhaling the musky scent of sex and sweat. He eased out of Cal and rolled to the side. He needed to get rid of the condom and clean them up, but that would involve energy, and Seth wasn't sure he'd have any anytime soon.

He felt Cal tremble, then tense beside him. He then heard a smothered sound, and his own body tensed. *Was Cal crying?*

"Cal, baby. What's wrong? Did I hurt you?"

Another smothered snort came from the man beside him. Seth pushed up on his elbow to stare down at the amused face of his husband. Yes, amused. Not upset. No. Cal was trying not to laugh. *What the actual?*

"Wanna share the joke?" he asked gruffly, not more than a little hurt than having the man he'd just had the best sex of his life with laughing right afterwards.

Cal giggled, and then, obviously seeing something on Seth's face, bit his lip in an attempt to stop smiling, but amusement still danced in his eyes.

"I'm sorry," he said between giggles. "I'm not laughing at you or anything you did, I promise." He laid a hand on Seth's cheek. "It's just that I'm not sure that when the doctor said to keep my foot elevated, he meant over my husband's shoulder as he pounded my ass...." Cal broke off into another fit of giggles, and Seth couldn't help but join in.

"I'm sure he didn't," Seth agreed. He ran a hand along Cal's thigh. "I didn't hurt you though, did I?"

"No, you didn't," Cal reassured him, giggles now under control. "I can't feel anything below my waist."

Seth ran a hand over Cal's belly and soft cock, which twitched at the gentle touch. "How about we get cleaned up, and you take some painkillers so that when this post-orgasm glow wears off, you're not sore?"

"In a second," Cal whispered, wrapping a hand around Seth's nape and pulling him close. Their mouths met in a slow, sensual kiss that sent a warmth through Seth and wrapped itself around his heart.

CHAPTER EIGHTEEN

C al stretched like a lazy cat before snuggling back into Seth's chest. Warm air brushed across his shoulder as Seth gave a soft snore as he tightened his arms around Cal. His body was soft and pliant. The tenseness and stiffness in his shoulders was all but gone, thanks to the hour-long massage he'd had yesterday at Sunny's wellness retreat and, of course, the sex he and Seth had indulged in upon their return home.

This was something he could get used to, waking up with Seth every morning. In all honesty, it may have only been two nights, but he really couldn't imagine sleeping in a bed without Seth there, and that meant trouble.

How had he fallen so hard and so fast? Yes, he'd only met Seth five months ago, and their interactions had been brief, and generally business related. The few times they'd been in social situations—when the band and crew had dinner and drinks or fun outings like the laser strike competition—he'd stayed away from Seth, not wanting to let his crush shine for all to see.

Wil and Sam had teased him, but it had been a gentle poking. He'd had a few texts from both, wondering where he was and if he was going to join them gaming online. He'd messaged back and told them about his foot and that he was just taking time to heal and that he'd be back soon.

For the first time in a while, his fingers itched to get behind a keyboard to do something. To lose himself in code, seeing magic appear from the strings of letters and commands he created. Of course, though, all his gear was at Sarge and Jax's place on the other side of the city.

"That was a big sigh." Seth's sleep-roughened voice was low in his ear. "What's ticking through that sexy brain of yours?"

"Sorry, didn't mean to wake you," Cal replied, turning to face Seth. He smiled at the sleep-rumpled man, his faux hawk sticking up in ways it certainly wasn't meant to. Cal ran a hand through the dark blond locks, trying unsuccessfully to tame it a little.

"You didn't," Seth said, rubbing his eye with the heel of his hand. "And I wouldn't complain if you did. I enjoy waking up with you."

"Funny, I was just thinking the same thing."

"Oh, were you now?" Seth's smile turned decidedly wicked. "And were you also thinking about doing something about this?" he asked as he slipped a hand between them to grasp both of their cocks.

Cal moaned, and heat pooled in his groin, stiffening his cock. "Well, I wasn't, but I am now."

An hour later, sated from their frotting session in bed and a shared shower, Cal took a mouthful of his coffee and sighed in contentment. The scent of the fresh espresso was a balm to Cal's soul, and he closed his eyes and inhaled again.

"If you're getting that much enjoyment from a cup of coffee, I have to presume my brother is not doing his husbandly duties properly?" Art's voice broke into Cal's reverie, making him jump in surprise, eyes flying open to see him grinning in front of him.

"What? No! I mean...." Cal stammered.

"What do you mean, 'no'?" Seth growled from the doorway. "You were shouting my name not an hour ago."

"Are you sure he was shouting in pleasure, or just at you because you've come between him and his espresso, because I've got to say, Seth, it could be either."

"Fuck off, Art," Seth said, pushing his brother out of the way. "Tell him, babe. Tell him just how good I've been at my husbandly duties."

Cal snorted at the by-play between the two siblings. He batted his eyelids. "A gentleman never tells, especially before he's finished his coffee."

"Babe! I'm wounded," Seth pouted. "If we weren't already married, I'd marry you just so we could keep having the incredible sex we're having."

This time Cal's snort was a choke as his mouthful of coffee sprayed across the table. Both men looked on in concern, but Cal waved them away. Grabbing a napkin from the holder on the dinette table, he wiped his mouth and then used another to clean the table.

"Cal, you can confide in me. I am a lawyer, after all. Is Seth lying? Is he that bad in bed?" Art laid a hand on Cal's, keeping a remarkable poker face, although Cal could see the humor dancing in his eyes.

"I'm not sure how that pertains to the case, Mr. Worthington," Cal replied, arching an eyebrow.

"Well, I can get you out of the marriage. An annulment. Irreconcilable differences." He dropped his voice to a whisper. "Just say the word, and I'll release you from this life of misery."

Cal grinned and leaned forward, beckoning Art closer. In a low voice, he whispered, "Sorry. Best sex of my life. I ain't goin' nowhere."

"Well, damn," Art sighed. "Oh well, just thought I'd make the offer. You know where I am if things change. You're still in the honeymoon stage after all."

"We're good, thanks Art." Cal patted his hand, before catching Seth's eye over his brother's shoulder and sending him a wink.

Seth grinned back at him before turning his attention to his brother. "So, apart from casting aspersions on my sexual prowess, why are you here, Art?"

"I hadn't heard from you in a few days, so I thought I'd pop in and make sure everything was okay, and to let Cal know I've heard from Systems Corp."

"You have? What do they have to say for themselves?" Cal carefully lowered his coffee mug to the table, his hand not quite steady. Seth slid into the booth beside him, wrapping an arm around his shoulders.

"Oh, there was a bit of to-ing and fro-ing. Claims of misfiled paperwork. Blaming of staff who no longer worked there. But once I told them we would file a damages case, they were suddenly very accommodating, and amazingly, all the 'missing' paperwork suddenly appeared."

"What does that mean?" Seth asked.

"It depends on Cal," Art replied.

"What depends on me? I signed everything I had to. They waived the non-compete clause, and even if they hadn't, I've not been in the business since they got rid of me, so they can't use that against me. System Corp is at fault. They're the ones who haven't honored the contract." Anger and hurt welled up in Cal. How dare they mess him around like this for months, and then have the audacity to throw it all back in Cal's court?

"They've agreed to pay you out the full sum they owe, plus another three months' pay in compensation for the pain and suffering you've endured."

"As they should. In fact, they should pay triple what they owe him," Seth raged, color high in his cheeks.

"I pushed for more, and there's still a chance they'll pay it, but they also made an offer to Cal."

"An offer? What kind of offer?" Cal asked, his curiosity piqued.

"They've been having some issues with one of their games. One you worked on, I believe, and they want you to come back to fix it."

Cal slumped in his seat, leaning heavily against Seth, who ran a soothing hand down his shoulder.

"They treat him like shit, fire him for no reason other than to save money, and now their prize jewel is failing, they want him back to fix it for them. Have I got that right?" Seth's voice radiated with anger. "Well, they can't have him."

"Don't you think Cal should be the one to make that decision?" Art replied, not at all fazed by his brother's outburst.

"Babe? What do you think?" Seth asked him, gently gripping his chin, so they were facing each other. Concern and something that Cal thought looked a little like fear were etched in Seth's features. "You don't have to do anything you don't want to do. I know you're bored and want to do something useful, but please, don't take this first opportunity just because of that. We'll figure something out for you, I promise."

Cal pressed a kiss to Seth's lips. "I know, and I understand your concerns. I'm not going to do anything stupid." He turned back to Art, who was watching them with a small smile.

"What are the terms of the offer?" he asked.

"They'll reinstate your employment with full staff benefits and a ten percent increase in your salary."

"This is on top of the payout they should have already paid, right?"

"Yes," Art nodded. "They're sending me the full offer today by email, but I wanted to come and feel you out first."

Cal sat back and mulled over Art's words. It was a generous offer. One he dreamed about... six months ago. Now, though?

"I'd like to think about it. Is that okay?"

"Yes. As both your lawyer and your brother-in-law, I advise you to take as long as you need. I'll forward everything to you once I've gone through it. You have a read and let me know what you think. If you have questions, etcetera, I can go back to them."

"Okay. Thanks, Art. We'll do that. I really appreciate your time on this. Are you sure I can't pay for your services?"

"Nope, you're family now," Art told him, with a wide smile. "Besides, you've put that look on my brother's face, and that's payment enough."

"Look? What look?" Seth demanded.

Art leaned across the table and patted Seth's cheek, none too gently. "You look happy, baby brother. You look happy."

***

Happy? Was he happy? Art's words from that morning danced around Seth's brain. He wasn't unhappy. He rarely was, so he wasn't sure what Art had been implying earlier. The soft tones of his guitar faded into the quiet air of his studio as he stopped strumming.

Art had stayed and had breakfast with them before heading to his office, promising Cal he would have the Systems Corp offer as soon as possible. Cal had been preoccupied and twitchy, ushering Seth off to the studio so he could have time to think things through.

He was pleased that Art had sorted things out with Cal's previous employers, but the thought of Cal going back to work for them didn't sit right with him. He wasn't sure if it was the thought of them screwing Cal over again once they'd gotten what they wanted out of him. Mind you, Art wouldn't let them. He'd have Cal's back every step of the way.

He knew Cal was bored, and he was realistic enough to realize that boredom and Cal didn't go well together. Hell, he hated having nothing to do himself. Even just a few days away from the tour, when he's supposed to be resting, he was here in his music studio rather than his art studio, noodling around with chords and riffs.

He laid the guitar down and slumped onto the couch. If he was honest with himself, though, it was more the thought of Cal not being around every day that bugged him the most. Of course, he knew that was ridiculous. There would be times when they'd have to be apart, but he liked the idea of having his husband with him on tour, and if Cal was working for someone else, then he wouldn't be able to travel with Seth. The idea of being apart for months made Seth decidedly *unhappy*.

It wasn't just the sex either, even though that was out of this world. He'd heard Cal's whispered confession to his brother earlier about it being the best sex he'd ever had, and he didn't think Cal would lie about something like that, even as a joke. He liked how Cal could make him laugh, even during sex, which was a first. His compassion and empathy were endearing, and he wasn't a bad cook either, whipping up a chicken dish the night before that Seth would have paid good money for in a five-star restaurant. Seth groaned. And now he'd made Cal sound like a nineteen-fifties housewife!

He liked the way his stomach dipped every time Cal walked into the room and caught his eye. He loved the sense of home and peace he felt whenever Cal was around. When he was upset, Seth wanted nothing more than to wrap him in bubble wrap and hide him away from the world. The thought of that all being taken away left Seth feeling hollow and sick.

Seth groaned as realization hit. He was falling in love with his husband. That's what Art had meant this morning. He'd wanted to say love, but he'd said happy instead so as not to frighten Cal away. *Well, shit!* What was he going to do now?

CHAPTER NINETEEN

C al finished reading through the Systems Corp offer for the third time and pushed it to one side. As promised, Art had sent it over by email and Cal had printed it out in Seth's home office, wanting to make notes as he read. As Art had said, it was a generous offer, one he'd be silly not to seriously consider it. But he just wasn't sure, and if one thing Sarge had drilled into him over the years, it was trust your gut.

Thinking of his cousin sent a twinge of guilt through him. Other than a couple of brief calls and texts, he hadn't seen Sarge or Jax. His fingers drummed on the tabletop, mulling over an idea. Coming to a decision, he tapped out a message to Sarge to see if he and Jax were home. He could see them to reassure them he was fine, and pick up his stuff while he was there. Two birds, one stone.

His phone buzzed with a reply, Sarge confirming they were home and to come for dinner. Shuffling the offer papers into a folder he snagged in Seth's office, he wondered where his husband was. Seth had mentioned something about the music studio, and Cal decided to look there first.

Swinging on his crutches, he headed down the hallway that led off the back of the kitchen towards the other side of the house. This place really was a rabbit warren, and Cal didn't really understand why Seth needed such a big place. Sure, he needed somewhere with privacy and security, but Jamie lived just across the valley in a very modest house with just as much security and privacy.

He soon came to a door that was ajar, and hearing the soft strum of a guitar, he quietly nudged it open to peer inside. Seth was sitting on a couch, an acoustic guitar on his lap, and he was humming and strumming quietly. At Cal's entrance, he looked up, and a huge grin spread across his face, sending a curl of warmth through Cal.

"Hey," Cal said, leaning against the wall. "I didn't mean to interrupt."

"You're not. I'm just playing around. Have you finished reading through the offer?"

"Yeah."

"And?" Seth stood and crossed the room to return the guitar to its stand. "Are you going to take it?"

There was something in Seth's tone that Cal couldn't quite put a finger on. Like he was interested in what Cal's response was, but also as if he was dreading what Cal might say.

"I don't know. There's just something niggling at my brain, and I can't put my finger on it. I'm going to let it stew for a few days, see what happens."

"Okay. That's cool," Seth nodded in what Cal hoped was understanding. "So, what do you want to do now?"

"I was wondering if you'd drive me to Sarge and Jax's place? I need to see them, and I want to pick up some of my gear too. If I'm going to be living here for the next year, then I really need my stuff out of their spare room."

"Yeah, sure. I can do that."

"I mean, I can always drive myself if you're happy to let me borrow the car. You don't have to if you're busy. I can call Sarge and ask him to drop it over here if that's easier."

"Do you have a car? Is it still over at Sarge's place?" Seth asked, frowning. "I should have thought to get it over here, so you're not stranded."

Cal felt the heat rise in his face. "Ah. I had a car. It was a bit of a bomb, but it got me from A to B when I needed it to. I... ah... had to sell it when I lost my job and couldn't make my rent." He dropped his gaze to the floor. He was so embarrassed to admit to Seth what a failure he was.

The warmth of Seth's body surrounded him as he stepped in front of Cal. Strong fingers tipped his chin until he was looking into the deep blue pools of Seth's eyes.

"Babe. Don't be embarrassed about doing what you had to do to survive, okay? I'm so mad that you had to go through all of that. Do you really want to go back to working for a company that treated you like crap?"

"No, not really. But I feel bad that *Runaway Donkey* is failing."

"Oh, Cal. That big heart of yours is going to get you into trouble one day," Seth told him with a smile.

Too late, thought Cal, even as he gave Seth a small smile.

"Um, Jax invited us for dinner, if that's alright?"

"Of course. When do you want to leave?"

"Soon. Traffic isn't going to be nice whenever we leave, so we may as well just head out and get it over with."

"Sure. Give me ten minutes, and then we can go." Seth pressed a brief kiss to his lips. "Everything will work out, Cal. Believe in yourself."

Twenty minutes later, they were wending their way towards the freeway, Cal relaxing into the soft leather seats of Seth's Range Rover. Yesterday they'd taken Seth's Maserati Gran Turismo, which Cal had quietly drooled over. Unfortunately, it didn't have the room for hauling his stuff back like the Range Rover did.

They idly chatted as they made their way across the city, Cal learning a little more about his husband.

"So, how did Sarge and Jax take the news of our marriage?" Seth asked, his tone casual, but Cal could see a fine line of tension in his shoulders.

"Didn't you talk to them in Denver?"

Seth shot him a sheepish grin. "I... ah may have kept out of their way as much as possible. Thankfully they were both so busy wrangling the Jamie and Kellet situation, that they barely acknowledged my presence."

"Oh, well then," Cal said with an evil grin, "expect to get the *'hurt him'* speech from Sarge, and try not to forget he's a former Marine, so his threats aren't suggestions. They're promises."

"Great," Seth muttered.

Cal reached over and patted Seth's thigh reassuringly. "Hey, don't worry. They know the truth about our marriage. Besides, after working with them both for so long, surely you realize it's actually Jax you need to be more worried about."

Seth grasped his fingers, not letting him move his hand. "I know, but this time I'm seeing them as their cousin's husband, rather than as one of the guys they wrangle."

"It'll be fine. Stop worrying."

Seth just huffed in reply and concentrated on driving.

When they finally arrived, Cal found himself suddenly nervous. *What if they didn't like Seth?* Then he mentally kicked himself. They already knew Seth. They already liked him. Sure, Seth tested their patience, but he hoped they would look past the rock star persona he donned and see the caring, considerate man that Cal was falling in love with.

In fact, that's what was probably unsettling him; given that Sarge and Jax knew him so well, they'd easily spot that Cal had fallen for the man he'd married.

After parking in a guest spot in the apartment garage, Cal used his swipe card to access the elevator. They quickly rode up to Sarge and Jax's fourth-floor apartment.

He knocked at the door, trying not to smile as Seth fidgeted beside him.

"Relax," he said.

At the sound of the lock being disengaged, Seth took a visible deep breath and plastered what Cal knew to be his PR smile on his face. Cal gave an internal groan, disappointed that Seth didn't feel he could be himself here.

The door opened to Sarge, grinning at them as he ushered them in. Cal had barely made it through the door before he was engulfed in his cousin's arms, Sarge's hug tight and warm.

"It's only been a week since you've seen me," he laughed as he extricated himself. "It's not like I've been gone for a year in Antarctica."

"We've been worried about you," Sarge said, holding his shoulders and running a keen eye over him. "How's the foot? Are you healing up okay?"

"The foot is good, thanks. The doctor said I can move to a cane in the next day or so, as long as I don't overdo it."

Sarge looked like he wasn't too happy with that decision, but before Cal could say anything, he'd turned his attention to Seth, who was hanging back quietly.

"Seth," Sarge greeted him, holding out a hand. "Good to see you."

"Hey, Sarge. Good to see you too."

An uncomfortable silence descended on the entranceway, and Cal rolled his eyes.

"Oh, for fuck's sake!" Jax's voice sounded from the other end of the apartment, and Cal looked at his cousin in askance.

"She's having technology issues. Can you see if you can help her out, please?"

"Ha! I knew there was an ulterior motive for asking us to dinner. You just want me for my IT skills," Cal teased. He glanced between the two men. "Play nice," he said before heading towards the study where he knew Jax would be.

***

Seth cleared his throat, shoving his hands deep into the pockets of his leather jacket. "Let's get it over with, Sarge."

"Get what over with?" Sarge asked, crossing his muscular arms across his chest.

"I promise I will not intentionally hurt Cal. We're two consenting adults that willingly entered this arrangement." He tried to convey as much sincerity into his voice as he could. "I really like and admire him. He's a great guy."

Sarge nodded. "Strangely enough, I believe you. For all your pranks and fucking around you do, you're an honest guy." He held Seth's gaze. "But if I even so much as hear a whisper of you looking at another person while you're with him, or you disrespect him in any way—"

Seth waved a hand at him. "Yeah, I know. Cal already warned me. You're a Marine. There won't be enough left of me to identify the body."

Sarge barked out a laugh. "Well, he's not wrong, but there are things worse than a pissed-off Marine coming after you."

"Yeah, he warned me about that, too." He nodded towards the apartment. "Shall we go and find your lovely wife?"

Dinner was pleasant once Seth relaxed. Jax had surprised him by hugging him, thanking him for looking after Cal when he injured himself. The conversation was light, the three of them sharing stories with Cal about life on tour and some of the crazy fans they'd dealt with over the years.

Seth had enjoyed watching Cal's face as he laughed, a radiant glow emanating from him. After the stress of the last few months, Seth thought he was finally seeing a side of Cal that had been missing for a while. Even Jax commented on it.

"You're looking a lot happier, Cal. I know we weren't onboard about this marriage arrangement, but I can see now how stressed you actually were about your job and money situation." She turned to Seth. "Thank you for helping him. You're a good man, Seth."

Unexpected pleasure washed through Seth at Jax's compliment. He smiled back at her. "It's really no hardship at all. He's helped me out, too, so it's a win-win situation."

"What's the plan for next week?" Sarge asked as he cleared their plates from the table. "Are you coming back on tour with us, Cal?"

"I... I don't know," Cal said, looking wide-eyed at Seth. "We haven't discussed it, really. I mean, I can still do some things, but running around an arena isn't really going to be possible."

"True," Jax agreed, tapping her lip with a bright red fingernail. "You're the only one that seems to be able to get the damned scheduling program to work decently. I mean, look at tonight. I'd been struggling for an hour to get it to sync from my laptop to the tablet, and within ten minutes, you'd had them talking like long-lost siblings."

"Seth, what do you think?"

"About Cal coming back on tour with us?" he asked. At Jax's nod, he sighed. "I'm the wrong person to ask. I want him to stay home and rest his foot and heal properly, and now that he doesn't have to worry about money, just take some time for himself. On the other hand, I want my husband on tour with me. I don't want to be away from him."

Jax blinked at him, surprised.

"What? Why are you looking at me like that?"

"Like what? I'm just realizing that there's more to you, Seth Worthington, than you let everyone see."

Seth gave an embarrassed cough and dropped his gaze. Cal's warm hand covered his, and he glanced up to see his husband giving him a knowing smile.

He squeezed Cal's fingers and shot a grin at Jax. "Yeah, well, don't start spreading rumors. I've a reputation to uphold."

"Your secret's safe with me," Jax replied with a wink. "Now, Cal. Let's get your shit boxed up. Are you taking everything?"

Seth watched Cal as he followed Jax down the hallway, loving the way he chattered and tried to talk with his hands, even though he was balancing on crutches.

"You really do like him, don't you?" Sarge's voice dragged his attention away from how Cal's butt looked in his jeans as he swung on his crutches.

"Yeah, Sarge. I do," he replied softly and honestly. If he was to be taken seriously by not only Cal but his family too, then he needed to let them in behind his walls.

CHAPTER TWENTY

"That's the last of them," Cal said as Seth settled a box onto the desk in the mansion's home office.

"In the morning, we'll get online and order you a desk," Seth said, looking around the room thoughtfully. "There's more than enough room in here. Change everything around to suit yourself and order whatever you need to get up and running."

"I don't want to kick you out of your space," Cal's protest was quickly cut off by Seth gathering him in his arms and kissing him. Thoroughly.

"Babe, in case you haven't noticed, we're not short on space around here. If this room doesn't suit you, then pick another. The only rooms off limits are the recording studio, my art studio, and our bedroom." The last was said with an eyebrow waggle.

Winding his arms around Seth's neck, Cal gave him a mock pout. "Oh, so I can't redecorate the bedroom with animal print wallpaper and velvet cushions."

"What color cushions?" Seth teased.

"Orange, of course." Cal rolled his eyes. "I mean unless you're partial to lime green or fluorescent pink."

"Ah. No. I like our bedroom as it is, thank you very much. The only change I'm happy with in there is you, sprawled naked across the bed."

Cal shook his head. "No. Can't visualize it. I think you're going to have to give me a demonstration."

He gave an unmanly yelp as he was suddenly scooped up, bridal style, and he clung to Seth's wide shoulders, laughing as he was carried from the room.

"Stop. You'll drop me," he gasped.

"I will if you don't stop wriggling," Seth warned him as he carefully made his way up the stairs.

Cal stopped moving but let his fingers tickle gently at the nape of Seth's neck below the heavy fall of silken hair.

Once in the bedroom, he was carefully lowered to his feet. Seth held his arms as he got his balance, trying not to put too much weight on his foot.

"Now what?" he asked.

"Now, I'm going to peel every layer of clothing off you, then you're going to lie across the bed, and I'm going to taste you from head to toe."

A shudder went through Cal at Seth's words. "And then what?" he asked huskily.

"Why don't I show you?"

***

Seth rolled over, reaching for Cal's warm body. Instead of a soft and well-sated husband, he found cool sheets and a crumpled pillow. He sat up, pushing his hair out of his face, glancing at the digital clock on the bedside table. Two-thirty am. Where the hell was Cal?

Worry flickered through him as he pushed back the covers. He quickly found his boxer briefs that had been discarded earlier on, and after pulling them on, checked the bathroom first. Okay. He thought Cal would have woken him if he was ill, so it probably wasn't that.

He made his way downstairs. He didn't want to call out and scare Cal, just in case he was sleeping on the couch. As he got to the base of the stairs, he heard a noise coming from the office. His heart thumped with a sudden adrenaline strike as panic shot through him. The exterior alarm system would have activated if there was an intruder. He shook the errant thought from his head. It wouldn't be an intruder.

Wishing he'd picked up his phone, he crept over to the half-closed door. There was a dim light emanating from the room, and he cautiously poked his head around it. Relief flooded through him, making him sag against the wall as he found Cal behind the desk, muttering to himself as he scribbled on a legal pad.

Seth blinked. When they'd left the office a few hours ago, there had been a stack of boxes and computer equipment, all carefully packaged. Now, there were piles of discarded bubble wrap and partially emptied boxes, their contents spilling out onto the floor.

On the desk were three large computer monitors, their screens lit up, casting Cal in an unearthly glow. A tangle of cables and cords stretched across the room, a hazard that would give Californian Health and Safety officers a heart attack.

Not wanting to startle Cal, he knocked lightly on the door. Cal's head sprang up, eyes wide until he saw who was watching him. A guilty flush flooded his skin.

"Hi. Sorry. Did I wake you? I tried to be as quiet as I could."

"No, you didn't wake me. The empty bed woke me." Seth gestured to the desk. "I thought after two orgasms you'd be dead to the world, not plotting world domination in the early hours of the morning."

"Sorry. They were very good orgasms, too. You were amazing, as always. I just couldn't get my brain to switch off. It's been so long since I wrote any code, and something Jax said sparked an idea, and until I get it down, I'm not going to relax and sleep."

Seth carefully picked his way across the room, stopping to lean against the desk and looking at the screens. Now he was closer, he could see several discarded sheets of yellow legal paper covered in letters and numbers that made absolutely no sense to him.

"What's all this?" he asked, gesturing to the mess on the desktop.

"You know how we've been having issues with the scheduling program. How long it takes to sync, and don't get me started on all the things I wish it could do, but doesn't?"

"Yeah," Seth said. "I know Jax and Miles have cursed it more than once, and Liam gets this look in his eye when he can't get the information he wants, when he wants it."

"Well, I couldn't stop thinking about it, and then I got an idea, and then..." he sighed and gestured to the office. "The next thing I knew, I was down here, unpacking boxes, trying to find power outlets, and setting everything up."

"It couldn't have waited until morning? Or at least until a slightly more human hour than three am?"

Cal yawned, eyes watering. "No. Don't you ever get a piece of music or a lyric stuck in your head, and you have to get it down? Or you see something you just have to draw. Right then? Well, that's what code is like to me."

"Okay. I can understand that." He pulled Cal out of his seat, wrapping his arms around him. "It's also why I have a notebook in the bedside drawer, so I don't have to leave my warm bed, or my husband, to pursue it."

"Normally, that would work for me too," Cal said, another yawn overtaking him. "Okay. I think I can sleep now." He pressed a kiss to the underside of Seth's jaw. "Take me to bed?"

"Always," Seth agreed. "But you only get carried once a night, so you're on your own getting back up those stairs."

"Piggyback?" Cal asked hopefully.

With a groan, Seth kissed him quickly, before turning around for Cal to climb on his back.

CHAPTER TWENTY-ONE

C al stared blindly at the code scrolling across his screens, mind wandering. After being carried back to bed, he and Seth had slowly made out, too tired to do anything more than kiss and snuggle against each other as sleep gradually took them over.

When they'd woken at a much more decent hour, they exchanged blowjobs in the shower, before Seth had headed off to his art studio, leaving Cal to finish sorting out the office and translating his ideas into workable code.

He'd flicked a text to the group chat that included all the band, Jax, and Miles, asking for their wish lists in the scheduling system. He'd had some good suggestions, plus instructions from Miles to log his hours for whatever he was creating so they could reimburse Cal for his time.

Sunny and the dogs had popped in earlier, Lulu and Trixie as exuberant as ever, licking at every possible body part they could reach on Cal. In turn, he had showered them with tummy-rubs which had Sunny rolling her eyes at their antics.

After a brief chat, she'd left Cal to his work, telling him she'd be in the kitchen making lunch, and to call for her if he needed anything.

The sound of knocking at the front door startled him. *Who the hell could that be?* He knew Jamie and Kellet were heading back to Jamie's place today, after spending most of the week at Kellet's place in Juniper, but he didn't think they'd call in unannounced, and they hadn't heard from Liam all week.

A muffled curse from Sunny as she crossed the foyer had him frowning. That was so not like Sunny. She lived up to her name, rarely cussing and always with a smile on her face. Grabbing the cane that was leaning against his desk, he rose and crossed the room to peer around the door.

"What are you doing here, Donald?" she asked, her tone cold and withering. "You know Seth doesn't like it when you turn up unexpectedly."

"Well, if my son bothered to let us know he was in town, we would let him know we were coming to visit. As it is, we were in the area and decided to call in on the off chance he was here."

Sunny gave an inelegant snort. "A likely story. What do you want?"

"Belinda, stop playing gatekeeper and let us in. We know Seth is here, and we want to see him."

Belinda? Who the hell was Belinda? Cal wondered. From what he'd heard, he figured Seth's parents were here. He wasn't sure what to do. Should he make himself known? Did they know about him? Did they know that Seth had gotten married?

Sunny sighed heavily and stepped back to let a well-dressed couple enter. Seth's father, Donald, was tall, with dark hair, graying slightly at the temples. His suit was well-cut and high-lighted his broad shoulders. Next to him, a woman with high-lighted dark blonde hair and a pinched face looked around the foyer with disdain.

"If you'd like to wait in the sitting room, I'll find Seth for you," Sunny told them as she ushered them into one of the more formal rooms that led off the foyer. "Would you like coffee?"

"Yes, please," Seth's mother replied, barely looking at Sunny as she passed her. Cal's hackles rose. How dare they treat Seth's aunt like that, and in Seth's home, too? He waited until they were in the sitting room before sneaking out of the office and hobbling as fast as he could to the kitchen.

"Sunny," he hissed, "is that Seth's parents?"

She nodded grimly, pulling coffee pods out of the drawer. "Yes, that is my delightful older brother, Donald, and my insufferable sister-in-law, Elaine."

"Why do they want to see Seth? Does he know they're here?"

"I just sent him a text message. He's not happy, but he'll be here in a moment. He'll need a minute or two to get himself in the right frame of mind to deal with them."

"Deal with them? Are they really that bad?" Cal cast a worried glance over his shoulder, hoping that neither of them were nearby.

Sunny sighed, carefully placing the coffee cups she held onto a serving tray. "Cal, it may be better if you stay in the office, out of sight."

"Why? I mean, I understand Seth probably hasn't had a chance to tell them about us, but would they really disapprove of our marriage?"

"Cal, honey. They disapprove of *everything* in Seth's life. You and your marriage will just be another thing to add to the list."

Cal stared at her, not sure what to say. Before he could formulate anything, the back door swung open, and Seth stormed in, tension radiating off him.

"Where are they?" he growled at Sunny. "And what the fuck do they want?"

"In the sitting room, and I don't know. Do you want me to call Art?"

"I've already called him. He'll be here as quickly as he can."

Cal reached out a hand, grasping Seth's arm. "What can I do to help?"

Seth's gaze softened for a second, and he leaned forward to press a quick kiss to Cal's mouth. "Nothing, babe. Stay here or in the office. I don't want you poisoned by them."

Disappointment and hurt flickered through Cal. He wanted to support Seth, show him that he wasn't as fragile as he sometimes appeared. "Okay. I'll just go back to the office."

He gave Seth's arm a reassuring squeeze and then turned away. He was halfway across the foyer when the sitting room door swung open, and Donald Worthington strode out. They both stopped in surprise.

"Who are you?" Donald asked, running his eyes up and down Cal, his gaze lingering on the cane clutched in his left hand.

"I... I'm Cal," he said simply, not wanting to engage.

"And what do you do here, *Cal*?" The way Donald said his name had Cal's spine stiffening. "Are you another of my son's conquests? I'm surprised to find you here. He rarely brings anyone back here and never for more than one night."

"Don't you speak to him that way," Seth's voice thundered across the foyer. "Who I have in my home is my business. And right now, Cal is a damned sight more welcome here than you are, *Father.*"

Cal flinched at Seth's tone. He'd never heard the level of anger before, and he hoped he never heard it again. Seth's hand settled on the small of his back, and Cal welcomed the touch.

"Donald? What's going on?" Elaine Worthington stepped out from behind her husband, coming to a surprised stop when she saw Cal and Seth. "Oh. There you are, Seth." Her glance raked up and down Cal. "And who is this person?"

Cal gripped his cane tighter. He'd never felt so put down by just a simple question.

"Shit," Seth said under his breath. Cal glanced up at him and gave him a small smile. Seth quirked an eyebrow back, silently asking if he was going to be okay with whatever came next. Cal hoped his slight nod reassured him.

With a deep sigh, Seth continued. "Father, Mother. This is my husband, Callahan Stevens. Cal, these are my parents, Donald and Elaine Worthington."

"Husband?" Elaine questioned. "What do you mean by husband?"

Cal bit back a grin. She seemed confused by the word.

"Like what Father is to you, Mother," Seth drawled sardonically.

"But how? When?"

"Shall we go and sit, rather than doing this in the foyer?" Sunny asked, appearing with a tray laden with coffee cups.

Elaine turned on her heel and stormed into the sitting room. Donald followed suit, and Sunny grinned at them both as she passed.

"Do you want me to join you?" Cal asked. "I can stay in the office if you want me to?" He really didn't want to hide in the office, but from the stress lines on Seth's forehead, he really wanted to do what was best for Seth. And if that meant hiding away, then he would.

"No," Seth sighed. "They'll only be offended that you won't make time to visit with them." He pressed a kiss to Cal's temple. "But please, don't take anything they say to heart, okay. They're spiteful and vindictive and only see things their way."

"Okay." Cal stretched up and kissed Seth. "Thank you for warning me."

Seth entwined their fingers and led Cal to the sitting room where his parents sat waiting.

***

Seth led Cal to one of the cream couches before sitting down beside him. He looked at his parents, who sat opposite and got a reassuring wink from Sunny as she handed him a coffee. He relaxed a little at his aunt's gesture. He knew she would have his and Cal's back.

"So, you're married?" his father began. Seth nodded as he took a sip of his coffee. "And when did this fortuitous event happen?"

"A week ago, when we were performing in Las Vegas."

"Oh, so a quickie wedding, then?" Elaine said scornfully. "What is it you do, Mr. Stevens?"

"I'm a software designer and developer," Cal replied.

"Oh? You're rather young, aren't you? I thought you had to go to college to learn that."

Cal gave her a brief smile that didn't reach his eyes. His tone was a fraction tighter and colder when he replied. "Oh, Mrs. Worthington, I'm older than I look, and I hold a degree from MIT."

"And how did you meet our son?" Donald asked.

"Cal has been working with Jax for this leg of the tour," Seth started to say, before he was interrupted by his father.

"And what would a band need a software programmer for?"

"I'm developing a new scheduling system for the band that uses an interface that can be accessed by everyone from Miles right down to Cathy in craft services," Cal jumped in smoothly, before Seth could even formulate a reply. "You would not believe how complex the operation is, and Miles and Jax thought it was best if I join the tour and see all the behind-the-scenes workings to get a better understanding of what they require."

Seth eyed his husband at the lie. Where the hell had this confident man come from? Yes, Cal had been quiet and nervous around them when he first joined the crew, and as he relaxed, they'd seen the fun side of him, but this guy? Seth was impressed, and a little turned on.

His father looked a little non-plussed at the reply, but quickly regained his footing. "So, you haven't known Seth for long, then?"

"We met a few months ago, around the time Kellet rejoined the band, and we began rehearsals for this leg of the tour," Seth told him.

"The James boy?" Elaine asked with a sniff.

"Yes. Kellet James, our original drummer. I told you that Mark left the band, and we were able to convince Kel to come back and join us."

"I thought he was married with a child?"

"He and Andi never married, but they co-raised their son, Wil. Did an amazing job too. He's a great kid and joined Kel on tour as his assistant."

His mother dismissed the topic with a wave of her hand. "Why the urgency to get married if you've only known each other a short time. In fact, why get married at all?"

"We were there. It seemed like a good idea," Seth said with a shrug, not willing to give his mother any more information than required.

"Just seems rather hasty and spur of the moment to me," she continued. "What are you going to do once your tour is over?"

"What I always do. Come home, recharge my batteries and start work on the next album."

"Another album? I presume that will mean another tour. Surely, now that you're married, you'll want to settle down. Stay at home more and be with your... husband." The pause before 'husband' was slight, but Seth heard it.

"Mother, I am a professional musician. Writing and performing are what I do. While the fans still want to buy our albums and see us live, Larkspur isn't going to stop."

"But they will stop one day. What are you going to do then? You'll have to find something to do with your time."

Seth closed his eyes and took a deep breath, praying for patience. Next to him, he felt Cal stiffen, and he gently squeezed his arm, hoping to convey that he didn't want Cal to engage.

"There are several different options open to me, Mother. When the time comes, I'll have plenty to keep me busy."

"And what about you, Mr. Stevens? What will you do once this project is complete?"

"Oh, I have several business interests of my own, Mrs. Worthington. I can fit them around whatever Seth is doing."

A muffled snort came from the doorway, and Seth looked up to see his brother grinning at him. Relief washed through him. Reinforcements had arrived.

"Arthur, my dear," Elaine cooed, her entire demeanor changing as her eldest son entered the room.

Seth pushed back the familiar feeling of hurt that pricked at his heart. He couldn't remember the last time she'd spoken to him like that.

"Mother, Father," Art greeted their parents as he entered. "Aunt Sunny," he said, bussing a light kiss to her cheek. He clapped Seth on the shoulder as he passed his brother to air kiss their mother and shake their father's hand.

"What are you doing here?" Donald asked. "Shouldn't you be at the office?"

"I have some paperwork for Seth and Cal to sign and thought I'd hand deliver it."

"You should use a courier service or have an office junior do that kind of work. As the firm's owner and senior partner, you can't be seen swanning off to do lackey work. You certainly wouldn't catch anyone from my firm doing that."

"Yes, well, I have an excellent team that doesn't need me to micromanage them, and also, I don't give them work to do that I wouldn't do myself."

Seth threw him a sympathetic glance as Art settled into the armchair across from him, giving a slight eye roll as he did.

"Yes, well, I prefer to be more traditional in my approach," Donald spluttered.

"We know, Father," Art said wryly.

There was a painful silence, and next to him, Cal fidgeted uncomfortably. Seth decided that was enough parent time for now.

"So, Mother, Father, I'm sure you've got busy schedules, and I know Art needs us to get this paperwork signed." He rose to his feet. "Thank you for stopping by. I'm away again in two days and will be home again late August."

His mother looked affronted at the dismissal, but Seth just arched an eyebrow at her. They'd had no reason to call by, other than the opportunity to remind him how he was wasting his life. They'd seen he was alive. Their time was up.

"I can see them out, Seth," Aunt Sunny said, smiling at him. "You and Cal go and do what you have to do with Art."

"Really, Belinda, you're not his housekeeper," Elaine said witheringly.

"Well, I kind of am," Sunny replied with a bright smile. "I look after things when Seth's not around, so technically, that's a housekeeper."

"You're a god-send, Aunt Sunny," Seth told her, the love he felt for her obvious in his voice. "I'd be lost without you."

Cal rose to stand next to Seth, using his cane to push himself up.

"Are you injured, Mr. Stevens?" Elaine enquired, her gaze snagging on his left hand where his wedding band shone brightly.

"I slipped over the other day and bruised the ligaments in my foot. Nothing major. More of an inconvenience, really." He nodded at Seth's parents. "Thank you for calling in. It was... nice to meet you."

He reached up and kissed Seth on the cheek. "I'll be in the office." Cal's green eyes shone with concern, and Seth squeezed his hand in thanks before watching Cal leave the room.

He nodded to his parents. "Shall we?" he asked, ushering them towards the foyer.

They'd almost reached the door when his father paused and looked back at his sister. "Belinda, I trust you'll be joining us for dinner on your birthday?"

Sunny shook her head. "No, Don, I won't be. I have other plans."

"In that case, we'll see you on Rose's anniversary."

"Again, no, you won't. I'll remember our sister in my own way."

"But, we're family. We should be together to honor her."

"And we will, in our own ways."

"For God's sake, Belinda, it's been three years. Surely you can put old history behind us."

"Goodbye Donald, Elaine." With that, his aunt turned on her heel and left the foyer. Seth flicked a glance to Art, who was looking as worried as Seth felt.

He pulled open the door. As he was about to bid his parents farewell, his mother gasped and looked at him with a calculating look on her face.

"Three years," she said simply.

"Three years, what?" Seth replied, acting dumb. He knew exactly what was about to come out of her mouth, and he braced himself for it.

"It's been three years since Rose passed. You only got married to get her money."

His father looked between his wife and his son. "Is this true, Seth?"

"Of course it is," his mother declared. "How convenient, a quickie marriage in Las Vegas. He knew what the date was, and he knew he needed to marry to meet Rosemary's will. Who is

Mr. Stevens really? I bet he's just someone you met in a bar and drunkenly decided to marry. He looks like the type to be on the lookout for a quick buck. Really, Seth. Have you no shame?"

White hot anger flooded through Seth. If it wasn't for his brother's restraining hand on his shoulder, he may have forgotten all of his upbringing, and punched his mother.

"Mother! That is totally uncalled for," Art said, placing himself between them. "How could you say such a thing? I was there for the ceremony. I handled *all* of the paperwork, and I can assure you, Seth and Cal married for love."

"I hope a prenup was signed," his father said.

"There was, in fact, at Cal's insistence. He rejected just about everything that Seth offered. He is not a gold-digger, so you can get that thought out of your head."

"Well, it's a sizeable amount of money. We have every right to be concerned."

Seth gave a humorless laugh. "Mother, I know you don't have any interest in my music, deeming it beneath you, but if the house and my car collection didn't give it away, I. Am. Successful. Aunt Rose's money is nothing but interest for any one of my investments. Once it comes through, it will all be donated to charity, as it should have been in the first place."

"I don't know what she was thinking with her bequest," his mother twittered on, ignoring Seth as usual.

"I don't either. I certainly didn't ask for it. Now, please leave. I don't have the energy to discuss this any further."

With that, he strode away, leaving his brother to ensure their parents left the property.

CHAPTER TWENTY-TWO

From his position by the office door, Cal watched as Seth strode across the foyer and towards the back of the house. The tension radiating off him could have triggered a minor earthquake, and Cal wasn't sure what to do.

He'd heard the terse exchange by the door and had been tempted to intervene. Thankfully, Art had skillfully stepped in. From what he'd witnessed this afternoon, he now understood Seth a lot better and his heart went out to the man he married.

"You okay, Cal?" Art asked wearily as he joined him in the office after seeing his parents out. Dealing with his parents had visibly drained him of all energy, and Cal felt for both brothers. Their parents definitely seemed like hard work and emotionally draining vacuums.

"I'm fine," he reassured Art. "Should I go after Seth?"

"No, leave him be for a little while. He'll be down in the gym beating the hell out of the punching bag. I'm really sorry you had to deal with them." He gave Cal a wry grin. "I'm impressed with how you dealt with them, though. I got here in time to see the way you jumped in and told them that story about developing a program for the band was genius."

Cal blushed. "Well, it was stretching the truth a little. I mean, I didn't want them to know that I was only working for the band because my cousin took pity on my sorry ass. But, as of this morning, I am working on a program for the band."

"You are? That's great. So, does this mean you've decided to reject System Corp's offer?"

"No, not yet. I'm still deciding, but we saw Jax and Sarge yesterday, and it sparked an idea, and I couldn't get it out of my head, so I started planning this morning."

"Okay. Let me know in the next couple of days what you decide and then we can go back to them."

"Thanks, Art. I really appreciate everything you're doing for me." He shot a worried glance towards the front door. "Your parents won't cause any problems, will they?"

Art sighed heavily, running a hand down his face. "No. They shouldn't, and if they do, Seth will just cut even more contact with them. He does the bare minimum as it is now. I'm actually surprised he saw them today."

"They turned up out of the blue. He didn't have much choice."

"Sounds about right." Art glanced at his watch. "Damn, I need to get going. I don't like to leave Seth after one of our parents' run-ins, but I have a charity thing I have to go to."

"Go. I'll go and find him shortly. If I need you, I'll call. I promise."

"Thanks, Cal. You're a good man. Seth could certainly have done a lot worse than marrying you."

Cal watched Art leave and decided to head to the kitchen. He needed another coffee and a few minutes to gather himself before he went and found his husband.

He found Sunny sitting at the dinette, nursing a small glass of whisky. He raised an eyebrow, and she smiled ruefully, with a wave towards the cupboard.

"Top shelf, help yourself. You probably need one too."

Cal decided he did, and after pouring himself a glass, went to join her at the table.

"So…" he said. "Those are the in-laws."

"Yep! How those two managed to turn out two fine men as Art and Seth, I'll never know. If it wasn't for the fact they both take after my brother in looks, and I saw Elaine pregnant with both of them, I'd be sure they were adopted."

"Have they always been like that?"

"No. When we were kids, Don, Rose, and I were inseparable. There's only two years between us, and Donald doted on his baby twin sisters. As we grew older, we still hung out together. There was never any of the usual sibling rivalries. We shared the same friends. We did everything together."

"What happened?" Cal was curious how such loving siblings could change into the people he saw today.

Sunny sighed and took a sip of her drink. "Don met Elaine at college. At first, she was wonderful. The typical girl-next-door. She joined in everything we did, not at all put off by our closeness. They got engaged his senior year, and when she graduated two years later, they got married. Don got a good job with a well-respected firm, and she was a secretary for a small engineering company. They wanted to wait to have children, which was fine. It gave Don time to establish himself in his firm."

"Then, Rose met Henri. Henri was the eldest son of a well-respected wine family that was looking to expand here in California. It was love at first sight, and they were engaged within weeks of meeting."

"How did you feel about that?" Cal asked.

"Oh, I was so happy for them. I wasn't ready for all that marital bliss. I've always been a free spirit, but back then, I was just a hippy-girl."

Cal chuckled. "Is that how you got the name Sunny? I was confused when your brother called you Belinda."

"Actually, our father nicknamed me Sunny. He said my smile was so bright, it shone like the sun. He used to call me his "sunny-bee"; a play on honey-bee. It stuck." She smiled sadly. "Don used to call me Sunny too, but that changed over time as he and Elaine began playing an elaborate game of keeping-up-with-the Joneses."

"What do you mean?" Cal asked.

"Henri was rich. Very rich, and although he never flaunted it, he and Rose had the best of everything. Nothing was too good for her. He doted on her. Elaine was jealous of, well, everything. The house they lived in, the clothes she wore, and the cars they owned. Don was doing okay. He made junior partner quite early on, and they had Art, who was the sweetest baby. Remind me sometime to pull out the photo albums."

Cal grinned. "Oh, I will, don't you worry."

"Two years later, Seth came along, and we thought Elaine might settle down a little, with two young children to look after, but she didn't. It didn't help that try as they might, Henri and Rose couldn't conceive. They had all kinds of medical treatments, but to no avail. They even trialed one of the first IVF treatments, but sadly it ended in a miscarriage."

"Despite having two beautiful children that she'd been able to conceive and carry herself, Elaine was still jealous of the attention Rose was getting."

"Did Rose and Henri not consider adopting?"

"They did, but after the last miscarriage, Rose became quite depressed and decided that motherhood wasn't for her. Henri took her back to Italy for a year to recuperate, and it helped somewhat. When they returned, she was back to her happy self, and doted on Art and Seth."

"That's so sad. From how Seth has spoken of her, she was an amazing woman." He reached over and laid his hand over hers. "You are too. Art and Seth are the men they are because of you and your sister."

Sunny gave him a watery smile. "Thank you, Cal. That means a lot to me. I was also never blessed with children. My attempt at marriage ended in divorce after a year when I found him cheating with his best friend's wife. I never met anyone else I'd consider having a child with, so like Rose, the boys became my boys."

She continued. "As Don went further up the ladder, the worse Elaine got. They moved to Juniper when Art started Junior High, as Don's firm opened a branch up there and he was senior partner. Elaine jumped at the chance to have a big house and the perceived social standing that came with being the lead partner's wife."

"As the boys grew older, Art was interested in what his father did and decided pretty early on he was going to be a lawyer. Seth was always more arty than academic. Elaine encouraged his interests at first, but when he started to talk about doing an Arts degree in college, she withdrew her support. When he met Liam and they started playing music together, she told him he had until the end of high school to live out his rock star fantasies and then he had to choose a good college and pursue a proper career."

Cal felt sick to his stomach. No wonder Seth hid himself behind a wall.

"That's when Miles found them, wasn't it?" he asked. He'd heard the story of how Miles had stopped in Juniper to listen to a high school band that had been recommended to him. He'd liked what he'd heard and worked with them to get a record label deal.

"Yes, and thank god he did. Not being able to create music or art would have killed Seth. Both my sister and I offered to pay for whatever college he wanted to go to. He wouldn't have had to rely on my brother, but his pride wouldn't let him accept it." She finished her drink. "I think that's enough reminiscing for one day. You need to go and find your husband and shower him with love. That's all he's ever wanted, someone to love him for him."

***

Seth gave the punching bag one last hit before dropping his hands. His chin fell onto his heaving chest as he fought off the anger and frustration that still coursed through his veins. *When was he going to learn? When was he going to ignore their toxic bullshit?*

His breath came in a half-sob, and he wiped his face with the back of his hand. The stray tear that had escaped was banished as quickly as it had appeared. He unstrapped his hands, throwing the soiled wraps into the hamper on his way out of the home gym.

He didn't see anyone as he headed upstairs to his room. His only goal was to get under a pounding shower.

As the steaming water enveloped him, his mind played over the visit from his parents. He knew better. He shouldn't let them get to him, but it was hard to break the habit of a lifetime.

So lost in his thoughts, he barely registered the shower door opening, startling when Cal's slim arms wrapped around his waist. The younger man didn't say anything, just pressed a soft kiss between Seth's shoulder blades before resting his forehead on his back.

They stood like that for a while, the water thrumming over them. Cal's thumb stroked the skin in the center of his chest, as if trying to soothe away his heartache.

He reached up and clasped Cal's hands in one of his. "I'm sorry," he rasped out.

"For what?" Cal whispered back.

"For subjecting you to them."

"I don't care about them, Seth. They're nothing to me." Another kiss to his wet skin. "Are you okay?"

"As okay as I'll ever be. I know I need to cut them out of my life—"

"But that's hard to do when all you want is their love and approval."

A sob rose in Seth's chest. He hated Cal could see that in him. That's what his walls were about, so no one could see that Seth was really just a lonely kid inside, waiting for his parents' acceptance.

Cal squeezed him tighter. "It's easy to say the words, *'you don't need it or them',* but in practice, it will take time and patience. And I'll be with you every step of the way, if you want me to be."

Did he? Seth wasn't sure he could share himself like that. He had Art and Sunny. What more did he need? Cal was silent behind him, letting him sort his thoughts out. No pressure. No pushing for an answer. Just letting him be.

Could he let this man further into his life, further into his heart? The feeling of quiet acceptance from Cal, right now in this moment, was a healing balm to his battered emotions. He pulled Cal's knuckles to his mouth and kissed them, his finger tracing over the bright gold band.

"You're willing to stick around, even though I'm a thirty-seven-year-old man with the emotional maturity of a toddler?"

He felt Cal smile against his back. "I happen to like thirty-seven-year-old men who sometimes act like toddlers. Besides, you're kinda stuck with me for a year."

"You don't have to stay married to me, Cal, if you don't want to. You can keep the money. I certainly don't need it, and I won't hold you to Aunt Rose's archaic bequest. The terms were that I only had to be married for a year. It never specified that we had to be living together for that year. Getting married has kept the money out of my father's pocket."

Cal tensed behind him. Seth felt him pull away, and he tightened his grip on Cal's hands, preventing him from going.

"You... you don't want to be married to me anymore?" Cal's voice was quiet, almost drowned out by the shower.

Seth's heart squeezed painfully at the thought. "I do, but I don't want you to feel like you have to stay."

"And if I want to?"

"But why would you? I don't have much to offer you."

"Oh, Seth," Cal breathed, and the weight of him resting his head against Seth's back gave him hope. "I'm sad you can't see yourself as I see you. You're warm, funny, kind, generous, but you hide behind a façade of laughter and jokes, of being the 'bad-boy' of Larkspur."

Cal reached around him, switched off the water, and then turned Seth to face him. He cradled Seth's face in his hands, forcing him to meet his gaze.

Seth braced himself, prepared to see pity in the deep green eyes, but instead, he saw something warm and inviting.

"Seth Joseph Worthington, just over a week ago, I made vows in front of an officiant and your brother. Despite my situation and the way you bamboozled me into a quickie Vegas wedding, to quote your mother—"

"Let's not, please."

Cal grinned. "Despite my situation, and the way you artfully conned me into a marriage of convenience, when we just happened to be in Las Vegas, I wouldn't have agreed if I didn't really like you and want to be with you."

This time, Seth's heart fluttered for a different reason. "You really like me, huh?"

"I. Really. Do." Each word was punctuated with a kiss. "Will you let me show you how much I really like you?" he asked huskily.

Seth simply nodded and let Cal lead him to the bedroom.

CHAPTER TWENTY-THREE

A fter quickly drying themselves off, Cal pushed Seth onto the bed. "Lie on your stomach," he commanded. As Seth got himself situated, Cal returned to the bathroom to grab the bottle of massage oil.

He climbed on the bed, straddling Seth's hips. "I'm not as good as the guys at Aunt Sunny's, but I know enough to relax you."

"Anything you do will be great," Seth told him, getting comfortable.

Cal warmed some oil in his hands and then ran his hands over Seth's broad shoulders. The muscles were taut under his touch, and he took his time, making broad sweeping strokes down one arm, before returning to repeat the maneuver on the other side. He fell into a soothing rhythm, keeping his weight on his knees.

Slowly, Seth relaxed, the sheen of oil on his tanned skin shining in the low light of the bedroom. His breathing evened out, and a long, soft sigh escaped him.

"Still with me?" Cal asked, pouring more oil onto his hands.

"Hmm hmm," Seth hummed in reply.

Cal shuffled back, so he was sitting on Seth's thighs, giving him better access to his lower back and ass. He ran his hands down Seth's spine, and then split them at the small of his back, rubbing down each flank and returning up the back of his legs. His fingers teased at the inside of Seth's thighs, the muscles twitching as Cal ran his hands up over Seth's beautifully firm butt.

On the third pass, a small whimper sounded from the head of the bed, and Seth's thighs parted as much as they could, with Cal bracketing them with his own. Cal smiled to himself and increased the pressure of his strokes. He let his fingers dip into the edges of Seth's crease, teasing but not stopping.

"Cal, baby," Seth pleaded, hitching his ass up. Cal leaned forward and pressed a kiss under his ear.

"Whatcha want, babe?"

"You. Touching me."

Cal sat up again, dragging his hands down Seth's spine. "But I am touching you."

Seth gave a frustrated groan as Cal's fingers dipped again into his crease. "There. Touch me there. I need...." he broke off as Cal relented and pressed the tip of his thumb against his hole.

He rubbed back and forth, increasing and decreasing the pressure until Seth was all but begging. He pulled his hand away, receiving a filthy curse from Seth in the process, and leaned across the bed to swap the massage oil for the lube and a condom.

He waved them in front of Seth's face before leaning down to kiss him hungrily. He pulled away and sat up on his haunches.

"No condom," Seth said.

Cal paused. "Are you sure?"

Seth nodded, and the thought of being in Seth bare had him rock hard in seconds.

"Look at what you do to me, Seth," he demanded huskily, drawing Seth's gaze to his hard and leaking cock. He ran a hand up and down his length. "This is what you do to me, every day."

Seth's gaze greedily took him in, his hand reaching out to stroke Cal. Cal whimpered at the touch.

"I want this inside me, baby," Seth told him.

"God, yes," Cal agreed. He dropped the condom, snapped open the lube and dribbled some down Seth's ass crack. He followed the sticky trail with his fingers, this time pushing one into Seth, who arched his back, seeking more.

"Fuck, yes."

As much as Cal wanted to make this last, the tight heat around his fingers called to his aching cock. He worked another finger into Seth, wanting him as relaxed and as open as he could be.

As Seth began to hump the bed, Cal knew it was time to get inside him. He tapped Seth's hip. "Roll over, babe."

Seth did, bringing his knees to his chest, opening himself up for Cal.

Emotion pierced at Cal's heart. This man, who was so intent on hiding behind walls, was completely opening himself up for Cal. Letting Cal see him at his most vulnerable.

Cal positioned himself and then slowly eased in. Seth drew in a harsh breath, and Cal stopped in concern.

"It's good. Keep going," Seth told him, taking a deep breath and relaxing his muscles. Cal slipped in a little further. "You feel so good, baby."

Once Cal was fully seated, he leaned forward and kissed Seth deeply, trying to convey some of the emotion that was coursing through him.

"Move, baby. Please," Seth begged.

Cal did as he was asked, soon lost in the sensation of warm, silky heat. The room echoed with the sound of flesh slapping and soft moans as they both took their pleasure.

Seth reached for his cock, stroking in time to Cal's thrusts.

"That's it, babe. Show me how you work yourself," Cal encouraged, his gaze torn between watching Seth's shuttling hand and his face, which was flushed and twisted in ecstasy.

"Ungh, Cal. I'm close. Don't stop."

Cal couldn't have stopped even if a magnitude ten earthquake hit. His hips pistoned back and forth as he chased his release. Before he could warn Seth, he erupted, spilling deep inside Seth.

"Oh fuck. That... you...." Seth was muttering incoherently before he orgasmed, cum spurting over his hand and belly.

Cal gave one final thrust before collapsing onto Seth. Seth's arms wrapped around him, holding him tightly, shudders wracking his body.

As their heart rates returned to normal, Cal softened and slipped out of Seth, feeling sticky and well-spent. Pressing a kiss to Seth's damp skin, he made to get out of bed. Seth's arms tightened around him.

"Where are you going?"

"To get a cloth to clean us up."

"In a minute."

"Okay," Cal agreed. He was in no rush to move if Seth wasn't.

***

Seth absorbed the heat and weight of Cal lying across his chest. At some point, Cal had demanded to be let go so he could clean them up. Once done, he'd snuggled back in tight, tracing lazy circles on Seth's chest that sent warm tingles through his body. His own hand followed a similar pattern on Cal's back and shoulder.

"How are you feeling?" Cal asked tentatively.

Seth mulled over his thoughts. He certainly felt better than he had earlier, but that wasn't hard.

"I'm feeling better, but I know how quickly that can change where they're concerned," he admitted.

"Do you think, maybe talking to someone about them and your feelings might help?"

"You're not the first to suggest it," he sighed.

"So why haven't you done it?"

"I suppose I don't want to admit to everything they make me feel. Don't want someone to confirm how stupid it is that I'm in my late thirties and I still crave my parents' approval."

Cal raised up on one elbow. "Oh, Seth. It's not stupid. It's a natural reaction, especially when you see how they look at your brother. That would hurt anyone."

"Thankfully, Art has always defended me against them. He never took the fact they were proud of him and not me and rubbed it in my face. He and my aunts are my biggest supporters. I don't know what I would have done without them to support and encourage me."

"I like your brother. He's a great guy. I'm surprised he hasn't been snapped up yet."

Seth chuckled. "Oh, many have tried, but he's not a one-person guy."

"One *person,* huh?"

"Yeah, he's pan, like me."

"And how did your parents take that, having two pansexual sons?"

"Oh, they don't know Art is pan." Seth grinned evilly. "I so want to be a fly on the wall when they find that out. They disregard it with me, as it's all part of my 'rebel rockstar phase'." He made air quotes with his fingers.

"Neither of you has ever had the urge to settle down then. No long-term relationships?"

"No. It's harder for me. A lot of people think it's all glamorous, touring the world, a different city every night. But once they see the reality of plane, car, hotel, car, venue, car, hotel, car, plane, they suddenly decide that I need to settle down, stay at home more to be with them."

"Or, if they can cope with staying home while I'm away for months on end, they get suspicious. They see a picture of me with a fan, and suddenly I'm cheating on them. It's just all too much to deal with, so I haven't bothered."

"That must be hard," Cal agreed. "For what it's worth, I trust you implicitly."

Surprise shot through Seth. "You do?"

"Of course I do," Cal told him with a frown. "Why wouldn't I?"

"But we've not known each other long. How do you know I wouldn't cheat?"

"Well, there's no one hundred percent guarantee, and I suppose there will always be the possibility that you'd be tempted, but you're very loyal. Even now, when you want to hate your parents for what they do to you, your sense of loyalty isn't letting you."

Seth was silent. He wasn't sure how to respond to that. His usual default would be to brush it off, or make a joke, but that felt like a disservice to Cal.

"I haven't offended you, have I?" Cal asked, worry in his eyes.

"No, baby. You haven't." He pulled Cal in for a kiss. "Thank you."

"For what?"

"Just for being you. I know this started out as a marriage of convenience for us both, but I really do care for you, Cal." He paused, not sure whether to admit his true feelings. The gentle smile Cal gave him spurred him on. "I'm falling in love with you, Cal. I don't expect you to return the feeling, but if I'm going to become a better person, then I need to be honest with you."

Tears filled Cal's beautiful green eyes, making them shimmer. "I'm falling in love with you too. I tried so hard to hide my crush, back at the start of the tour, but the more I got to know you, the more I realized it wasn't just a crush."

Seth couldn't help the grin that spread across his face as joy raced through him. "Really?" he asked.

Cal nodded, his own grin matching Seth's.

"So, we're going to make a go of this marriage thing, yeah?"

"Yeah. You won't be getting rid of me in a year."

Seth pulled his husband closer and took his mouth in a slow and sensual kiss, trying to convey all of his feelings.

Chapter Twenty-Four

S eth climbed the stairs into the private jet that sat on the tarmac at the VIP side of LAX.

"We can leave now, I'm here," he announced cheerily.

"Actually, we can't, unless you can play two guitars at once," Jamie told him with a grin as he gave him a hug.

Seth glanced around the plane, suddenly noticing that Liam wasn't onboard.

"Wait, you mean I actually beat Lee here?" He whistled. "Wow, that's a first." He threw his bag onto a seat before giving Kellet a hug too.

"All set for the last leg, Kel?"

"I can't believe we've only got another six dates to play. The time's gone so quickly."

"That's what happens when you're old," Wil called out from the back of the plane. "Hey, Seth. Did you have a good break?"

"Hey, Will. Yeah, I had a really good break, thanks. What about you? Did you catch up with your friends in Juniper?"

Wil told him all about the escapades he'd got into in the brief five-day trip back to his hometown. "My friends are so jealous that I'm working with you guys."

"I bet they are," Seth told him, settling into his seat. He called over to Jamie, who was sitting as close as he possibly could to Kellet. "So, have you spoken to Lee over the break?"

"No. Apart from the odd comment in the group chat, we haven't heard from him at all."

"That's not like him." Seth shared a worried look with Jamie and Kellet. Movement at the front of the plane had him looking up, but it was only Jax and Sarge boarding.

"Guys," Sarge greeted them as he moved to the back of the plane.

Jax paused by their seats. "Liam and Miles are two minutes away. They got caught up in traffic but are nearly here."

"Thanks, Jax. We were getting worried. It's not like Lee to be late."

"No, that's more your department, Seth," she replied with a grin. "With you being here on time, can I presume you've maybe turned over a new leaf? Taken a time management course during your week off?" With her back to Jamie and Kellet, she winked at Seth.

Seth decided to play along. "I may have implemented one or two new things into my routine."

"Glad to hear it. I hope whatever has inspired you continues to do so."

"Oh, I've got a really good feeling that it will."

With a pat to his shoulder, Jax moved to the seat next to her husband.

"Hey, Jax?" Wil called out. "Is Cal not joining us?"

"No, sorry. His foot's still not healed properly, and he felt like he'd be more of a liability than an asset. He'll be at the final two concerts, though."

Wil groaned and pouted, and Seth felt like joining him. Through his shirt, he fingered the ring hanging from the chain around his neck. It had torn him apart to say goodbye to Cal earlier on and remove his ring. He'd promised Cal that as soon as he came offstage in two weeks, the ring was going back on and not coming off, ever again.

Cal had told him he understood. They'd agreed to tell everyone about their marriage at the after-party following the last concert. Jax had drafted a press release to get ahead of any rumors circulating, and Miles had agreed to releasing it once the tour was over.

Seth flicked a glance at Jamie and Kellet. He was sure they would only be happy for him and Cal, but he also knew that he was in for the ribbing of a lifetime when they found out.

A harried-looking Miles strode onto the plane, followed closely by Liam. Seth eyed his bandmate closely. There was something different about him. He looked subdued but didn't seem to have the same air of tenseness that he usually carried.

Liam smiled at his bandmates, giving them hugs, before settling into a seat across from Miles. Their manager was talking with Jax, but Seth caught the glance he threw at Liam. A faint blush colored Liam's face, and he busied himself with getting his AirPods sorted out.

Seth frowned as the flight attendant came to check they were all buckled in, before confirming with their pilot. What the hell was going on there?

Soundcheck in Seattle went well, and Seth was happy to be back on stage. Larry called out for a five-minute break while the sound engineers tweaked something, and he took the opportunity to wander over to where Liam was taking a drink.

"Hey, Lee. How's it going?"

"Feeling good. I think we're going to have a good show."

"I'm looking forward to being back on stage," Seth told him. And he was, but he was missing Cal. He kept looking into the wings or across the empty stadium for his husband. Whenever he saw Wil, he automatically looked for Cal before reminding himself that Cal was at home in LA.

"What did you get up to over the break? I expected you to call and come over for dinner at least once," Seth commented.

"Oh. Yeah. Sorry. I... ah, was on a kind of retreat thing. I've been feeling quite stressed out lately, and ah... um... Miles suggested I go more or less off the grid for the week to try and relax more." A flush stained Liam's face.

Normally, Seth would have teased him about both the retreat and the blush, but something made him stop. He felt like Liam had been through some things over the last week, just like Seth had.

"Hey, man. Why didn't you say something? You know we would have all been there for you. I know I come off as an asshole most days, but I'm always here if you want to talk."

"Thanks, Seth. Yeah, I know. One of the things I learned this week was to not be afraid to ask for help."

"You and me both," Seth muttered. Liam frowned at him, but Seth was saved from explaining by Larry calling for them to reset.

"Beer after?" he asked.

"Always," Liam replied, with a smile.

CHAPTER TWENTY-FIVE

C al took a deep breath to calm his nerves. Next to him, Art gave him a reassuring smile, adjusting his suit jacket. He looked every inch the professional lawyer he was. The elevator slid to a smooth halt, and the doors opened with a quiet whisper.

They stepped out into the brightly lit, stark white foyer of Systems Corp's head office. Cal tried not to appear overawed, but it was hard. Everything was sleek and shiny, a far cry from the slightly battered, worn offices that had housed Crinkle Media.

Art gave their names to the blond receptionist, who gave him a slightly less than professional smile. Art didn't react, either not noticing or ignoring her, instead stepping back to Cal's side.

They waited in silence as their names were passed back to whomever was meeting with them, and a few moments later, a dark-haired woman appeared and asked them to follow her. They were shown into a small conference room and told to help themselves to refreshments.

Wanting something to do, Cal got them both a bottle of water.

"I really wish they'd kept to the original meeting time," he said to Art as he took a seat next to him.

"Hmm," Art hummed as he took a slim folder from his brief-case. "I'm not sure if they're playing mind games, or if they actually had to reschedule because something came up."

Cal wasn't sure, but he didn't like it either way. He'd gone back to Systems Corp with a counteroffer, which they'd taken a week to mull over before responding. They'd agreed and asked that Cal come in to sign the paperwork. The meeting had been planned for the twenty-fourth, which worked out perfectly because Larkspur's final concert was the twenty-first.

The plan had been for him to join Seth at the band's hotel in central LA for the last two nights of the tour, and then he'd have the meeting with Systems Corp, sign everything off, and then he and Seth could get on with their lives.

But three days ago, Art had called him to tell him that the meeting had been changed to today. The twenty-first. Cal had tried everything he could think of to get them to change it back. He missed Seth and was desperate to see him again. It had been a long three weeks, and no amount of messaging and video calls could make up for being in his husband's arms.

The door opened, and Cal was surprised when Phil Harmon walked in, followed by another man who he didn't recognize.

He and Art got to their feet as Harmon held out a hand.

"Phil Harmon, lawyer for Systems Corp," he introduced himself. "And this is Mr. Bennet Tull, head of software development."

"Arthur Worthington, and I believe you know my client, Cal Stevens."

Harmon gave Cal a brief nod, which Cal returned.

"Thank you for coming in today," Tull said. "We apologize for changing the date. However, I have to fly to Japan this evening to visit one of our subsidiaries."

"We also have a prior commitment this evening, so if we can get down to business, we can all be on our way."

Harmon shuffled some papers in front of him. "Now, I understand, the original redundancy settlement was six months' salary and a waiver on the non-complete clause."

"That is correct, and my client signed the agreement at the time, eight months ago," Art said, his tone firm. "And as of today, he still has not been paid what he is owed."

"Yes, that is a terrible oversight on our part. There was no malice or intent to defraud Mr. Stevens. The paperwork got misfiled, and we are very sorry for the inconvenience it has caused," Tull replied, casting a sympathetic look to Cal.

"It is very unfortunate that it took so long to sort out, especially after Cal contacted your organization several times, to no avail. It was only after I contacted you that things seemed to be resolved."

"I think you'll find that we have offered a very reasonable damages package, which, for the most part, your client has accepted," Harmon blustered.

After seeing Art at work, smoothly efficient with a quiet air of ruthlessness, Harmon came across as a bumbling idiot.

"Yes, it is most generous, and like you say, Cal has accepted the terms for the most part. He has, however, made a request that you said you were happy to honor."

"We are," Tull jumped in before Harmon could reply. "Cal—may I call you Cal?" At his nod, Tull continued. "Looking over the work you did on developing not only *Runaway Mule,* but other programs, I am extremely disappointed that you were made redundant. You were certainly an asset we were foolish to let go of."

Tull's words warmed Cal, and some of the tension he'd been carrying since that horrible day eased. He wasn't one who normally needed validation, but his self-esteem had taken a huge knock, and hearing that they'd made a mistake in letting him go did a lot to replenish his soul.

"Thank you, Sir, that means a lot to me."

"Tell me, what can we offer to get you back? I need people like you on my team."

"Again, I'm extremely flattered, but one good thing to come out of the last eight months is that I met my now-husband. He travels a lot with his job, and I want to be able to be with him whenever possible, which would be difficult to do when I'd be required to be in a corporate office every day. That is why I suggested consulting for you on an 'as needs' basis."

"Congratulations on your marriage. I can understand your reticence to return to a position where the hours are long." Tull opened up the file in front of him. "You're offering your services in a consultant capacity, correct?"

Cal nodded. "Yes. I'm offering to consult initially for eight to twelve weeks—no longer—to go through everything that is not working on *Runaway Mule* and correct it. Once that is completed, I will be available for a set number of hours per month, to be determined on a case-by-case basis. Of course, this will have to be worked around other clients I'll be working with."

Bennet Tull's eyebrows raised at the mention of other clients but made no comment as he read further. "And you'll charge an hourly rate?" he asked as he got to the end of the proposal.

"We thought a fixed sum for the initial consult and then an hourly rate to be determined once that is completed," Art interjected. "We feel the offer is fair and commensurate with Cal's skills."

Tull hummed again before removing a pen from his jacket pocket. He scribbled something on the paper. Harmon's eyes widened as he saw what had been written.

"Mr. Tull, I really must advise—"

"Thank you, Philip. I have spoken with both the CEO and COO, and they gave me full permission to do what I felt was best to secure Mr. Stevens's services."

He pushed the contract across the table. Art picked it up, his eyebrows raising before he showed it to Cal. Cal read the handwritten numbers on the page. They were nearly triple what he'd requested.

"Um. Wow!" Cal said, extracting a chuckle from Tull.

"You're worth it, Cal. If you won't come and work for me directly, I want to ensure I am your number one client."

Cal looked at Art. They hadn't discussed this scenario. Art gave him a brief nod. Cal wanted to grin and do a small jig, but managed to keep himself relatively composed. Just.

"Thank you for your very generous offer, Mr. Tull. I'm happy to accept these terms."

Bennet Tull gave him a bright smile and handed him his pen. Cal nodded his thanks, and then slowly and carefully read through the contract again. He'd read it several times already, but he wanted to make sure nothing had changed.

Art gave a quiet chuckle beside him while Phil Harmon fidgeted impatiently.

Once Cal was satisfied and had received another nod from Art, he initialed the changes Tull had made and then signed with a flourish at the bottom of the page. Art witnessed his signature, and then they waited as Tull countersigned, witnessed by Harmon.

"Philip will ensure that these are filed correctly," he said pointedly, "and full payment made to your account for all outstanding monies." He glanced at his Rolex. "I really wish I didn't have to rush off, as I would have liked to have taken you out for a drink to celebrate."

"Unfortunately, we have to get across town to Jefferson Stadium, so we wouldn't have been able to take you up on that," Cal replied as they all stood.

"Well, when I'm back from Japan, my assistant will be in touch, and we can start ironing out these problems with *Run-*

away Mule, and we can maybe have a drink then." Although Tull was talking to Cal, his eyes drifted to Art briefly.

"I look forward to it," Cal replied.

"May I ask why you're heading to the Stadium on a Wednesday night? I wasn't aware of there being a game on," Tull queried as he escorted them to the elevator.

"There's a concert tonight," Cal replied. "It's the final night of Larkspur's world tour."

"I'd heard that sold out. You're lucky to have gotten tickets."

Cal smiled smugly as he entered the elevator. "Yes, we were very lucky." Cal held in his laughter until the doors closed, and then he was laughing so hard, he had to lean against Art.

"Oh, my God. Did that just happen?" he asked, wheezing.

"Yes, Cal, it did. Congratulations. That went better than I'd hoped."

Cal tugged at his tie. "Right, how quick can your driver get us across town? I need to see my husband before he gets on stage."

CHAPTER TWENTY-SIX

The crowd roared in response to Jamie's taunt that they weren't being loud enough, making Seth grin. He caught Liam's gaze and winked. His bandmate grinned back, nimble fingers plucking out the extended bass line to their first-ever hit. Even after sixteen years, it was still a crowd favorite and one that the band loved to play live.

Kellet added in the drumbeat, and then Seth picked up his cue, watching as Jamie stalked to the end of the stage, whipping the crowd into a frenzy. Seth sank into the familiar tune, eyes roaming the crowd at the front of the stage. He'd been desperately searching for Cal all evening. His husband and brother had not made it to the venue in time to see him before the concert started. He'd received several messages, each one getting more and more frustrated as Cal and Art had been caught in traffic caused by a pileup on the freeway.

He'd had to shut off his phone fifteen minutes before getting on stage, so he wasn't sure if they'd arrived in time to see the start of the show. He'd even asked Blue, his guitar tech, if he'd seen Cal when he'd run on stage to do a quick change during one of Jamie's chat sessions. Blue had shaken his head, and a tendril of worry had crept through Seth at the thought that something may have happened.

As his solo riff got closer, he moved to the edge of the stage, the fans screaming, he grinned cockily at them. Some held up signs—most fairly innocent—but one caught his eye, asking for a threesome. He made eye contact with the holder, hooding his lids and biting his lip, as if considering the suggestion, then gave a rueful shake of his head, and blew them a kiss at their mock pout.

He turned to the other side of the walkway that extended into the heaving masses, glancing down towards the VIP section where family and close friends were situated. He caught sight of Kellet's family and Jamie's parents. For once, the familiar pang didn't go through him at the lack of his parents' presence. He saw Mark, their former drummer grinning up at him, and he grinned back. His ex-bandmate looked a whole lot happier and healthier than the last time he'd seen him.

Standing just behind Mark, he finally spied Art, and his heart lifted. The cue for his solo came through his in-ear monitor from the sound desk, and he threw himself into it with gusto. If Art was here, then so was Cal. He couldn't see Cal in the crowd and managed to catch a hand signal from his brother waving towards the stage. He nodded in response. Cal was backstage. With a final flourish, he all but jogged back to his position on the main stage, mentally working out how many minutes exactly it was going to be until he had Cal in his arms again.

Thirty-eight and a half minutes later, following two songs, Jamie's extremely sappy thanks to everyone involved in the tour, another three songs, and an encore of yet another two, Seth slipped his guitar off for the final time for this tour. Clapping Blue on the shoulder in thanks, he unplugged his in-ears and tugged the wire out of the back of his shirt. As he descended the backstage stairs, he unclipped the transmitter and passed it to one of the sound engineers with a smile of thanks, his eyes searching desperately for Cal. He'd thought his husband would have been right there, but he wasn't.

He was accepting congratulations from Kellet's parents when he heard a shout from across the crowded backstage area. His head whipped round, and he opened his arms as Cal ran towards him, limping slightly, before jumping and landing right where he was supposed to be.

Their mouths met in a hot, wet kiss, and peace settled over Seth. They broke for air, grinning at each other. "Hey, baby."

"Hey, yourself. You were amazing up there tonight."

"Where were you? I couldn't see you." Seth asked, keeping his arms tight around him, inhaling the fresh scent of sunshine and lemons that he'd missed so much over the last three weeks.

Cal rolled his eyes. "Once the security guard finally accepted my credentials were real, I went and hung out in the sound booth, so I could have the best view of you."

"God, I've missed you. So much," Seth breathed, kissing him again.

"Umm, guys. Something you wanna share?" Jamie's voice had Seth reluctantly realizing where they were. He lifted his head, taking in the small audience gaping at them.

"Nope!" Seth replied. "I don't share." Jamie quirked an eyebrow. "That's all in the past. I'm a one-man guy now."

"So, you and Cal are together?" Kellet asked.

"What gave it away, Kel?" Seth asked, grinning, too happy to not be snarky.

"Seth!" Cal admonished, wriggling to get down. Seth tightened his hold. He didn't want Cal to go anywhere. Cal gave him a pointed look, and with a sigh, he loosened his hold and let Cal slide to his feet. He kept hold of him though, his arm around Cal's slim waist, fingers snuggly holding his hip.

"Yes, Seth and I are..." Cal paused, glancing up at Seth. Seth cocked a questioning eyebrow back. He was happy to let everyone know if Cal was. Cal nodded, and Seth hooked a finger inside his t-shirt, pulling out the thin chain that held his wedding ring.

Letting go of Cal, he undid the chain and let the ring slither into his palm. He held it out to Cal, who grinned as he took it and slid it onto Seth's left ring finger. He turned and held up his own left hand. "Yes, Seth and I are together. Forever."

Stunned silence greeted the announcement, before Wil almost shouted, "You got *married?*"

"We did," Seth confirmed, wrapping his arm back around Cal and pressing a kiss to the top of his head.

"Wow! Okay, this is very unexpected," Jamie began. At Seth's glower, he waved a hand. "Let me finish. It's very unexpected, but so very cool. Congrats, man." Jamie's genuine delight eased an unrealized tension in Seth, and he accepted his bandmate's hug.

"Thanks. It was quick and unexpected for us too, but it felt right, so we decided to just go with it," he said.

Kellet also gave him a hug before Liam stepped up. There was happiness in Liam's smile, but also a shadow in his eyes. He tugged his friend into his arms. "I'm here if you need to talk," he offered quietly.

Liam squeezed him back, just a little harder than was warranted for a congratulations hug. "Has married life made you a sap, Seth?" he asked as he released him.

"No, but it has made me realize that I don't have to face things alone. That I have a support network if I need it."

"Thanks," Liam said quietly, nodding. He gave Seth a soft smile before turning to hug Cal. "Welcome to the Larkspur family, Cal. You do know you're way too good for him, right?" he teased.

"Oh, totally," Cal replied, laughing as he side-eyed his husband. "But hey, beggars can't be choosers."

Seth gasped and pretended to tug at his wedding ring. "That's it. I want a divorce!"

Cal laughed and tugged him for a quick kiss. "Nope! You aren't getting rid of me now."

"Oh, yeah. Cal, you're going to fit into this crazy family just fine," Jamie told him with a grin.

"Okay, guys. Let's move this back to the hotel, yeah?" Miles said.

Hotel. Oh, definitely. Hotels had rooms. Rooms with beds. Rooms with beds and doors that locked. Seth met Cal's glance, desire coursing through him at the heated look Cal gave him. Yep. His husband was on the same page as he was.

"Cal, I need you with me when we get to the hotel, please," Jax called out.

What. The. Fuck? The glare both Cal and Seth sent her way should have had her cowering, but she simply raised a finely plucked eyebrow.

"Seth, you need to shower and change. If Cal goes with you, we won't see you until the middle of next week. You have obligations to meet at the wrap party. If Cal comes with me, and you promise to mix and mingle for a good hour, then you can disappear."

"I never took you for a cock-blocker, Jax," Cal grumbled. "Do you know how long we've been apart? You're mean, and I take back everything nice I've said about you."

"Three weeks is nothing," Jax parried. "Try being a military spouse when your Marine husband is deployed for a year. Then come talk to me about being sex-deprived."

Seth sighed and pulled Cal into his arms. "I'll have the quickest shower known to man, and we'll set a timer for the second we step into the party, okay?" With a thorough kiss, he let go of Cal and gently pushed him in Jax's direction. "I will not forget this, Jax."

"Consider it payback for all the years of hell you've put me through, Seth," she replied, tucking Cal's hand into the crook of her elbow.

"She's got you there," Jamie told him. "Come on, the quicker we go, the quicker you can start that timer."

CHAPTER TWENTY-SEVEN

"How much longer?" Seth murmured in Cal's ear, his warm breath sending tingles down Cal's spine.

"Only five minutes less than the last time you asked me," he replied. Seth groaned and buried his face in Cal's neck.

"Are you sure?" he whined.

Carding his fingers through the strands of hair that hung over Seth's collar, he hummed. "Yep. I know, babe. Who else do you need to talk to?"

"Just Larry, and then that should be it." Seth stood up straight and scanned the room, looking for their tour manager.

They'd made their way around the various crew members, Seth offering his thanks for a job well done. Many of the team had been with them since opening night in Australia, back in February.

Even though Cal had only been with the band for a few months, he was going to miss them all. Both Jamie and Liam had been right when they'd called it family. Despite not being around for the last three weeks, he'd been welcomed with open arms by everyone he'd worked with. They'd commiserated over his injured foot, and given teasing condolences on his marriage to Seth.

"There he is," Seth said, grabbing his hand and tugging him across the room to where Larry was talking with Miles.

"Larry, so glad you got here," Seth greeted him enthusiastically.

Larry snorted, not at all taken in. "Well, I got here as quickly as I could. You may have finished your bit, but there is still work to be done."

"I know, and I appreciate every one of the guys that have to stay back and break down the set," Seth responded sincerely.

"I understand congratulations are in order," Larry offered, nodding to them both. "And, Cal, I hear you're working some magic and developing a better management system for us."

Cal nodded. "Yeah. I've done the bulk of the programming. I just need to start some beta testing with Jax and yourself, and while you do that, I'll work on the graphics and pretty it up."

"You have?" Seth asked him in surprise. "I thought it would take a lot longer."

"It could have, but it's not like I had anything else to do, y'know, with my new husband being on tour and me being injured," Cal said wryly.

"What happened with Systems Corp?" Seth asked, and it was clear from the look on his face, he'd only just remembered why Cal hadn't been able to join him a few days ago.

"Really good. I'll tell you all about it later."

"It's been a good tour, and I'm proud to have been a part of it," Larry said. "You two go and catch up. I'll see you next week when we meet for the debrief."

"Thanks again, Larry. It wouldn't be as good as it was without you running the ship," Seth offered, giving the man a hug.

As Larry left them, Miles looked at them both. "The press release is going out in the morning. I'd suggest laying low for a few days, but I'm thinking that really won't be an issue?"

Cal laughed at the wry question. "No. We're staying here for a couple of days, then flying down to Texas to see my family. We'll be back after the weekend for the meetings."

"Meeting the parents? How do you feel about that, Seth?"

"From what Cal has told me about his family, they're gonna love me," Seth replied confidently. "Besides, they really can't be any worse than my own, and Cal has had the misfortune to meet them."

"You're right." He held a hand out to both of them. "Congratulations on a successful tour and your marriage."

"Thanks, Miles," they responded.

"Cal, I'm hoping you'll continue to work with the band?"

Surprise had Cal blinking at the man. "I'd like that," he replied. "I'm not sure in what capacity, but if it means I can be on tour with Seth, then yes."

"Don't worry, we'll find plenty for you to do. I've got a good feeling about this new package you're developing for us, and I have a few ideas for you. We can discuss them next week."

With that, Miles left them, leaving Seth and Cal alone.

"Okay, that's it. We've paid our dues. I don't care what Jax says," Seth told him, putting his empty beer bottle on a nearby tray. "If we sneak out that door, we can bypass the lobby and be back in our room in less than five minutes."

"I totally agree," Cal told him, twining their fingers together. "My foot's sore and I think I need to elevate it."

Seth's eyes darkened with desire, a small smile tugging at his lips. "Oh, you do, do you?"

"Hmm. Think the hotel has any extra pillows we can use? You know, to make sure it's in the right position."

Seth captured his mouth in a searing kiss. "We don't need pillows; I have the perfect spot for it."

EPILOGUE

*T*wo months later

Seth entered the house with a spring in his step, wondering if he could pull his husband away from his work early.

As expected, the faint strains of music came from the office, letting him know Cal was still entrenched in layers of code. Throwing his car keys onto the kitchen counter, he stopped briefly to pull two bottles of water from the fridge and a pre-prepared snack tray. He'd learned early on that Cal forgot to eat when working, so they'd come up with healthy snack trays he could graze on while he worked.

The door to the office was open, and Seth took a moment to take in Cal as he frowned at the screen, lips moving silently as he typed frantically. He still couldn't believe that this bright, beautiful man loved him and wanted to be with him.

He'd said as much to his therapist today, and she'd told him he deserved the love Cal gave him. He'd finally agreed with Cal, Art, and Sunny that he needed to talk to someone about the issues he had with his parents. He'd learned to not feel guilty for the way they made him feel. He was still deciding if he was going to cut them and their toxicity out of his life completely, or whether he was going to keep contact to the barest minimum.

Cal gave a sigh, slumping into his seat. Seeing the break in his concentration, Seth stepped into the room.

"Hey baby, how's it going?"

Cal's face lit up when he saw him, sending a shaft of warmth through Seth. It was something he'd never get sick of seeing.

"Hi! How was your session?"

"It went well. In fact, I've got something I want to talk to you about." Seth placed the snack tray on the very crowded desk before leaning down to kiss his husband.

Cal hummed in appreciation, tongue flicking into Seth's mouth.

"Love you," he murmured.

"I love you too," Cal returned, kissing him again.

The moment was broken by Cal's stomach rumbling, and Seth pulled back with a chuckle. "You forgot to eat again, didn't you?"

Cal nodded guilty, and Seth pushed the snack tray towards him.

"So, what did you want to talk about?" he asked between bites of a carrot stick.

"How do you feel about moving?" Seth watched him closely, waiting for his reaction.

Cal paused mid-chew and washed down his mouthful with a swig of water. "Move? As in, leave this house?"

"Yeah."

"I thought you loved this house?"

"No, not really. I mean, there are parts I love, like my music and art studios," he gave a brow waggle, "and our bedroom, of course, but I only really bought this place as a big 'fuck you' to my parents. To rub their noses in what I have." He hung his head. "Esther has made me realize that no matter what I do, they're never going to see me as successful. I could live in the White House, and it still won't be enough for them."

Warm hands tilted his chin up, and he met Cal's loving green gaze. "I don't care where we live, as long as we're together."

"Yeah?"

"Yeah. We can find a place that means something to both of us."

Seth kissed him, pouring all his love into it.

"Of course, it will have to have somewhere for Aunt Sunny to stay, and space for your studios," Cal told him.

"And a custom office for you," Seth told him.

Cal grinned. "Let's do it."

"I'll call some realtors in the morning," Seth told him, gathering him tightly into his arms.

"In the morning? Why not now? It's only early afternoon."

"Because we're busy this afternoon," he replied, nibbling down Cal's neck.

"We... we are?" Cal stammered as Seth hit a particularly sensitive spot.

"We are," Seth confirmed.

The End

ACKNOWLEDGEMENTS

T hank you for reading Riff. I couldn't do this without your support. Please consider leaving a review, even a short one. Reviews and ratings go a long way to help an independent author.

I started writing Riff in January 2021 after finishing Snare. I got to twenty-thousand words and Seth and Cal went quiet on me. It took until October of 2022, after I had completed my paranormal story, that they started talking again, and with the support and encouragement of my amazing editor, Penny, I finished writing in early January 2023.

A huge thank you to the team that helped bring Riff to life;
My beta reader, Megan Dischinger of Blue Beta Reading, for asking the questions that needed to be asked and that added an extra three thousand words to the manuscript. And going above and beyond in helping with the blurb.

Editor Penny Tsallos. Thank you from the bottom of my heart for all that you do, especially the things outside of your editor role. Your encouragement and check-in's keep me motivated and focused. I'm so happy that Angelique Jurd introduced us, although I'm not sure what you did to deserve two crazy Kiwi authors in your life, but you wrangle us with grace and aplomb.

Proofreader Corrinne Beehre – thank you for being a friend with an eagle eye.

Cover designer, Morningstar Ashley. I love the covers for this series. Your talent is amazing.

To the Gay Romance Reviews team – thank you for your services. You help make this crazy publishing world a little easier to handle.

ALSO BY ZOE PIPER

All of Zoe's books are available on Amazon

The Kiwi Guys Series
Winning Love's Lottery
The Sweetest Song
Igniting the Flame
Cinders (short story)

LARKSPUR SERIES
Snare
Riff
Reverb (coming soon)

STANDALONE NOVELLA
Meet Me at the Altar

PARANORMAL
Soul Bound: A West Mill Pack Novel

ABOUT THE AUTHOR

Zoe Piper is English by birth and Kiwi by choice, living in Auckland, New Zealand for over thirty years. She has had a long and varied administrivia career in many different industries from agriculture to the outdoor sports industry. She is a bookaholic who devours several books a week, and when not escaping into other authors worlds, she can be found staring at her screen trying to wrangle her own.

Connect with Zoe via Linktree